Style or not, he's as treacherous as a snake,
Faithful warned her.

Alanna touched the ember-stone under her shirt. "I know," she replied softly. "I just wish I had something to crush him with."

Give him time, the cat meowed. *He'll give you plenty to crush him with.*

Alanna frowned. "The problem is that by the time he does he'll probably be invincible."

True. Faithful yawned. *Fog's rising.* And with that he curled up and went to sleep.

Alanna watched the ghostly white tendrils rising from the river's surface, feeling very tired. "Just what I need," she yawned disgustedly. "I didn't think there'd be any fog tonight."

The mist rose quickly, smothering all the night noises. Everything sounded different: the river, the distant camp, even the nearby waterfall. Alanna's nose itched till her eyes watered. She felt like lying down right there and taking a nap. That would never do: she was on sentry duty! Something was very wrong; the itching of her nose meant sorcery. Should she go for help?

The rock striking her head settled the question. Alanna dropped, and the men who had crept up behind her in the fog chuckled grimly.

Song of the Lioness Quartet
by Tamora Pierce

Alanna: The First Adventure (Book One)

In the Hand of the Goddess (Book Two)

The Woman Who Rides Like a Man (Book Three)

Lioness Rampant (Book Four)

∾

And don't miss Tamora Pierce's new Tortall series:

THE IMMORTALS

available for the first time in paperback,
from Random House Fantasy in May 1997:

Wild Magic (Book One)

Wolf-Speaker (Book Two)

Emperor Mage (Book Three)

In the Hand of the Goddess

Song of the Lioness
Book Two

TAMORA PIERCE

Random House ⌂ New York

Copyright © 1984 by Tamora Pierce
Cover art copyright © 1997 by Joyce Patti
All right reserved under International and Pan-American Copyright
Conventions. Published in the United States by Random House, Inc.,
New York, and simultaneously in Canada by Random House of
Canada Limited, Toronto. Originally published in hardcover by
Atheneum, a division of Macmillan Publishing Company, in 1983.
Published by arrangement with Atheneum.
http://www.randomhouse.com/

Library of Congress Catalog Card Number: 84-2946
ISBN: 0-679-80111-1
RL: 5.7

Printed in the United States of America 10 9 8 7 6 5 4

To Tim—the shoehorn for my triple D-sized love
and
to George, Pam, and Denise—together we'll
go very fast and very far on little tracks

୶

Contents

In the Hand
of the Goddess

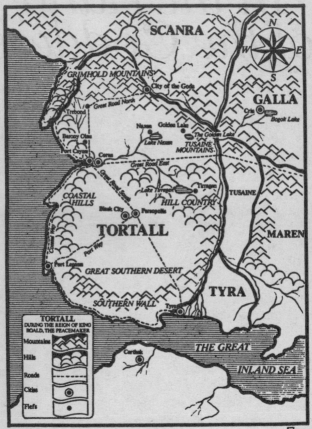

TORTALL
DURING THE REIGN OF KING
ROALD, THE PEACEMAKER

Mountains
Hills
Roads
Cities
Fiefs

SCANRA

GALLA

GRIMHOLD MOUNTAINS
City of the Gods

Cria
Bogok Lake

Great Road North
Trebond
Barony Olau
Port Caynn
Corus

Naxen
Lake Naxen
Golden Lake
The Golden Lake
TUSAINE
MOUNTAINS

Great Road East

Great Road South
Lake Tirragen
Tirragen
TUSAINE

COASTAL
HILLS
Black City
Persopolis
HILL COUNTRY

TORTALL

MAREN

Port Way
Port Legann

GREAT SOUTHERN DESERT

TYRA

SOUTHERN WALL
Tyra

Carthak

THE GREAT
INLAND SEA

Zaee

one

The Lady in the Forest

The copper-haired rider looked at the black sky and swore. The storm would be on her soon, and she was hours away from shelter. No matter what she did, she was going to have to spend the night out-of-doors.

"I *hate* getting wet," Alanna of Trebond told her mare. "I don't like being cold, either, and we'll probably be both."

The horse whickered in reply, flicking her white tail. Alanna sighed and patted Moonlight's neck—she also didn't like exposing her faithful mare to such conditions.

They were on the last leg of an errand in the coastal hills. A forest lay before them; beyond it was the Great Road South and a half a day's ride to the capital city and home. Alanna shook her head. They could probably find shelter somewhere under the trees, if luck was with them.

Clucking to Moonlight, she picked up their pace. In the distance thunder rolled, and a few drops of rain blew into her face. She shivered and swore again. Checking to make sure the scroll she carried was safe in its waterproof wrapping and tucked between her tunic and shirt, Alanna shrugged into a hooded cloak. Her friend Myles of Olau would be very upset if the three-hundred-year-old document she had been sent to fetch got wet!

Moonlight carried her under the trees, where Alanna peered through the growing darkness. If they rode too much longer, it would be impossible to find dry firewood even in a forest this thick. The rain was falling now in fat drops. It would be nice if she could find an abandoned hut, or even an occupied one, but she knew better than to expect that.

Something hit the back of her gloved hand with a wet smack—a huge, hairy wood-spider. Alanna yelled and threw the thing off her, startling Moonlight. The gold mare pranced nervously until her mistress got her under control once more. For a moment Alanna sat and shook, huddled into her cloak.

I hate *spiders,* she thought passionately. *I just— loathe spiders.* She shook her head in disgust and gathered the reins in still-trembling hands. Her fellow squires at the palace would laugh if they knew she feared spiders. They'd say she was behaving like a girl, not knowing she *was* a girl.

"What do they know about girls anyway?" she asked Moonlight as they moved on. "Maids at the palace handle snakes and kill spiders without acting silly. Why do boys say someone acts like a girl as if it were an insult?"

Alanna shook her head, smiling a little. In the three years she had been disguised as a boy, she had learned that boys know girls as little as girls know boys. It didn't make sense—*people are people, after all*, she thought—but that was how things were.

A hill rose sharply to the left of the road. Crowning it was an old willow tree thick with branches. It would take hours for the rain to soak through onto the ground under that tree, if it soaked through at all, and there was room between the limbs and trunk for both Alanna and Moonlight.

Within moments she had Moonlight unsaddled and covered with a blanket. The mare fed on grass under the tree as Alanna gathered dry sticks, branches and leaves. With some struggle and much swearing—her first teacher in woodcraft, Coram, was a soldier, and she had learned plenty of colorful language from him—she got a fire going. When it was burning well, she gathered large branches that were a little wet, putting them beside the fire to dry. Coram had taught her all this when she was a child at Trebond, planning to be a warrior maiden when she grew up.

There was only one problem with her ambition, Coram had explained when she told him what she wanted to be. The last warrior maiden had died a hundred years ago. Nobly born girls went to convent schools and became ladies. Boys became war-riors, particularly their fathers' heirs, like Alanna's twin brother Thom, who was often reading, gener-ally books about sorcery. Thom was no warrior, just as Alanna—who had the Gift of magic as well as he did—was no sorceress. She hated and feared her magic; Thom wanted to be the greatest sorcerer living.

Alanna frowned and took food from her sad-dlebags. She didn't want to think about Thom now, when she was tired and a little lonely.

She sneezed twice and looked up, sharply scan-ning the clearing beyond the screen of willow branches. When supernatural things were about to happen her nose itched; she didn't know why. And now the *feel* of the clearing had changed. Quickly she shoved the cloak back, freeing her arms. Searching the darkness with wide violet eyes, Alanna loosened her sword, Lightning.

Moonlight whickered, backing against the wil-low. "Something wrong, girl?" Alanna asked. She sneezed again and rubbed her nose.

A sound came from the trees behind her. She spun, unsheathing Lightning in the same move-ment. The sound was repeated, and Alanna frowned. If she didn't know better, she would swear something had *mewed* out there! Then she laughed, sliding Lightning back into its sheath, as a black kitten trotted through the branches sheltering her from the rain. It mewed eagerly when it saw her, its ratlike tail waving like a banner. Staggering over to Alanna, the tiny animal ordered her to pick him up.

The squire obeyed the kitten's command. Cuddling it against her shoulder, she searched her saddlebags for her blanket.

"How did you get here, little cat?" she asked, gently toweling it dry. "It's a bad night for *anyone* to be out-of-doors."

The kitten purred noisily, as if it agreed. *The poor thing is skin and bones—not someone's pet,* Alanna reflected. Wondering what its eyes looked like, she lifted its chin with a careful finger, and gulped. The black kitten's large eyes were as purple as her own.

"Great Merciful Mother," she breathed with reverence. Settling by the fire, she fed her guest as she thought. She had never heard of a *cat* with purple eyes. Was it supernatural? An immortal, perhaps? If so, she wasn't sure she wanted anything to do with it. She had troubles enough!

His stomach full, the small animal began to wash vigorously. Alanna laughed. Violet eyes didn't make a creature supernatural. Weren't she and Thom proof of that? This cat certainly behaved like a normal animal. Thinking of something, she lifted her new pet's tail and checked its sex. Satisfied he was a male, and ignoring his protests against the indignity, Alanna settled him on her lap. The kitten grumbled for a few moments, then settled himself.

She leaned back against the willow's broad trunk, listening to the animal's very loud purr. *It'll be nice to have a pet to talk to,* she thought sleepily.

The sneezes hit her, five at once, blinding her momentarily. Swearing like a guardsman, Alanna wiped her watering eyes. When she could see, a tall hooded stranger was standing beside her fire!

Alanna jumped to her feet, her sword unsheathed and ready, spilling the yelling cat to the ground. She stared at the newcomer, fighting to calm herself. She had no right to attack this— man? woman?—simply because she had been surprised.

"May I be of service?" she gasped. The kitten was tugging on her boot, demanding to be held once more. "Hush," she told it before looking at the stranger again.

"I saw your fire through the trees." The newcomer's voice was husky and soft, like the wind blowing through the treetops, and yet somehow Alanna was reminded of a pack of hounds belling in the hunt. "Would you permit me to warm myself?"

Alanna hesitated, then nodded. The stranger threw back the concealing hood, revealing a woman—the tallest woman Alanna had ever seen. Her skin was perfectly white, setting off slanting emerald eyes and full red lips. Her hair was unbound, falling loosely below her shoulders in black, snaky locks. Alanna gulped. The woman's face was too perfect to be quite real, and she settled before the fire with boneless grace. She watched Alanna as she sat down clumsily again, her amazingly green eyes unreadable.

"It is odd to see a youngling alone in this place," she said at last. Her mouth curved in a tiny smile. "There are strange tales about this tree, and what passes beneath it."

The kitten jumped back into Alanna's lap and purred. Alanna stroked it nervously, never taking her eyes away from her visitor.

"I was caught by the storm," she answered carefully. "This was the first shelter I found." *And now I'm sorry I found it*, she added to herself. *I don't like surprises!*

The woman looked her over carefully, still smiling that hooded smile. "And so, my daughter, now you are a squire. Within four years you will be a knight. That doesn't seem so far from now, does it?"

Alanna opened and closed her mouth several times with surprise before biting her lips together. The "squire" part was easy; beneath her cloak she was wearing the royal uniform, as was required when squires went abroad without their masters. But the woman had called her "my daughter"; the stranger knew she was a girl, even though she was dressed as a boy with her breasts bound flat! And her own mother had died years ago, when Alanna was born. Suddenly she remembered that she had heard the woman's voice before. Where? At last she made the safest answer she could.

"I don't want to seem rude, but I'd rather not speak of the Ordeal," she said flatly. "I'd like not to *think* of it, if possible."

"But you must think of it, my daughter," the woman chided. Alanna frowned. She had almost remembered… "When you undergo the Ordeal of Knighthood, many things will happen. You will become a knight, the first woman knight in more than a hundred of your years. You will have to reveal your true sex soon after that; your own nature will not let you remain silent for long. I know well how much you hate living a lie before your friends at the palace."

Alanna stiffened. She had remembered that voice. Jonathan had been a boy, dying of the Sweating Sickness. The palace healers said there was no hope, but Alanna—only a page then—had gotten Sir Myles to convince them to let her use her healing Gift. The sorcery causing the fever was too much for the magic she knew, and in the end she had appealed to the Great Mother Goddess. She had heard a voice that hurt her ears—a woman's voice that sounded like a pack of hounds in full cry, like the huntress urging them on. And she had heard that voice again, only a year ago, when she and Jon were trapped in the Black City. They had called on the Goddess for help then, and she had told them what to do.

"That's impossible," she whispered, her voice shaking. "You—you can't be—"

"And why not?" the Mother asked. "It is time we talked, you and I. Surely you know that you are one of my Chosen. Is it so strange that I have come to you for a time, my daughter?"

Life is difficult enough with the gods meddling in it, Myles had told her more than once. *But they will meddle. All we humans can do is hope they tire of their meddling soon and leave us alone!*

Alanna clenched her chin stubbornly. "I never asked to have conversations with the gods," she informed the immortal on the other side of the fire.

"Indeed, you ask very little." The Mother nodded. "You prefer to do all you can by yourself. But events for you in the next few years will determine your life's course, and you have no living mother to advise you." The kitten jumped from Alanna's lap and ran to the Goddess, mewing angrily. The woman picked him up in a graceful hand, stroking his fur with scarlet-painted nails. "She will be all right, Small One. She only needs a moment or two to adjust to her fear."

"I am *not* afraid," Alanna snapped. Emerald eyes caught and held hers, until she swallowed and looked away. "All right—I'm afraid. But it won't do me any good to give into it, will it? I mean, you're going to talk to me, and I can't prevent you, so I may as well accept it."

The Goddess nodded. "You learned your lessons as a page well," she approved. "But you have three fears that you have *not* accepted." When

Alanna said nothing, she went on. "You fear the Ordeal of Knighthood. You have feared it since you kept vigil during Prince Jonathan's Ordeal during this last Midwinter Festival."

Alanna looked into the fire. Seeing that it was burning low, she busied herself with putting more wood on the flames. In her mind she saw Jonathan stumble out of that iron-barred Ordeal Chamber, his face grey. He had looked at her without seeing her—Jonathan! Sometimes even now his eyes went dark and blank, and she knew he was remembering the Ordeal. Her voice shook as she said, "He looked like some part of him *died* in there. And then Gary had his Ordeal the next night, then Alex, and then Raoul—and they *all* looked that way." She shook her head, not looking at the Goddess. "They're none of them cowards. Whatever happened, if it was so bad for them—" She drew a deep breath. "Jon wakes up at night, *screaming* sometimes. And it's the Ordeal he dreams about, though he isn't permitted to tell me more than that. If the Ordeal is that bad, I won't pass it. I won't, and then it will all go for nothing: three years as a page, four as a squire, the lying, everything. It'll be for nothing." She stared into that unreadable face. "Won't it?"

"Prince Jonathan made you his personal squire, knowing you were a girl," the Goddess replied. "You have learned there is a world outside Trebond. You can ride; you can use a bow; you can fight with knife and sword and spear. You can read a map. You manage your fief through Coram while your brother studies. You can write and speak in two tongues not your own; you can heal one who is sick. I think you must answer your own question— is it worth what you have done?"

Alanna shrugged. "It is now. It won't be if I fail. Sometimes I wake up in the dark sweating, and I'm going to scream, except I don't. That would bring Jon into my room, and we agreed he shouldn't, not after we go to bed for the night. And all I can remember of the dream is that they're closing that iron door behind me, and I'm in the Chamber, and I can't see a thing."

"A dream is only a dream," the Goddess murmured as Alanna looked skeptical. She added softly, "Would it be so terrible if Jonathan *did* come to offer you comfort?"

Alanna blushed. "Of course it would. He—well, there's nothing like *that* between us. I don't want there to be."

"Because you fear love," the Goddess told her. "You fear Jonathan's love and the love of the Rogue, George Cooper. You even fear the love of Myles, who only wants to be your father. Yet what is there for you to fear? Warmth? Trust? A man's touch?"

"I don't *want* a man's touch!" Alanna shouted. Horrified, she put out her hands in a gesture of apology. "I'm sorry. I meant no disrespect. I just want to be a warrior maiden and go on adventures. I don't want to fall in love, especially not with

George or Jon. They'll ask me to give them parts of *me*. I want to keep me for myself. I don't want to give *me* away. Look at my father. He never really got over my mother's death. They told me when he died last month he was calling for her. He gave her part of himself, and he just never got it back. That's not going to happen to me." She drew a deep breath. "What's my third fear? I may as well hear it now and get it over with."

"Roger, Duke of Conté." The Goddess's voice was low, soft and deadly.

Alanna froze. Finally she said carefully (and very quietly), "I have no reason to fear Duke Roger. None at all." Then she put her head in her hands. "I don't have any *reason* to fear him—but I do." If she had doubted her visitor's identity, the fact that she was being so frank—almost against her will—convinced her. "I *hate* him!" she yelled suddenly, lifting her face from her hands. It felt good to say it, after all this time. "You know what I think? The Sweating Sickness. It drained every healer who tried to cure it. It struck only in the capital, nowhere else, and Jon was the last one to get it. They *knew* it had to be sorcerer's work. They sent for Duke Roger to help, but *none* of them—the King, Myles, Duke Gareth, Duke Baird—none of them thought Duke Roger might have created it! Thom says Roger is powerful enough to've sent it from as far as Carthak, where he was, and Thom ought to know." Alanna stood and strode around inside the shelter of the willow, her hands linked tightly in her belt. "When Roger tested me for magic, my head felt all funny, as if someone had been digging through my brain with a stick. Thom wrote me he was being watched up in the City of the Gods. And last summer—"

"Last summer?" the Goddess prompted.

"I don't think Jonathan would have gone *near* the Black City if Roger hadn't gathered us all to warn us about how dangerous it was. Jonathan's very responsible about being the Heir; he wouldn't risk his life foolishly. But Roger was wearing a great blue jewel around his neck. He twisted it while he talked to us, and the light bouncing off it made me sleepy, till I stopped looking at it. It seemed to me that Roger was talking only to Jonathan, *daring* Jon to go to a place where Roger knew he could get killed!" She sighed and settled back against the tree, feeling better than she had in a long time. "I can't say anything to Jon. I tried to, once, but he got angry with me. He *loves* Roger. So does the King. Roger's handsome, young, clever, a great sorcerer. *Everyone* thinks he's wonderful. No one stops to think that if something happened to Jonathan, Roger would be the heir. No one but me, that is."

"What will you do about this third fear?" the Goddess wanted to know. She shooed the kitten off her lap.

"Watch," Alanna said wearily. "Wait. Mostly watch him as carefully as I can. George—the thief—he'll help. Thom's helping, as much as he can." She had rarely felt this tired in her life. "And if Roger is what I suspect, I won't stop until I've destroyed him."

The Goddess nodded. "Then you are dealing with this fear, my daughter. Time will end your fear of the Chamber of the Ordeal, and your fear of love. Well, who knows what may happen to change your mind?"

"Nothing will change my mind," Alanna said firmly.

"Perhaps." The Goddess reached into the bed of the fire and drew out a single red-hot coal. "My time with you comes to an end. Take this from my hand."

Alanna swallowed hard. This was asking a bit much, even for a goddess. She looked up and met the Mother's eyes with her own. Slowly, trembling, she reached out and took the coal.

It was cold! Startled, she nearly dropped it. Looking at it, she saw that the ember seemed to burn within a crystal shell. There was even a tiny loop in the crystal, just big enough to permit a chain to pass through. The ember flickered in its shell, its hot red glare fading to a soft glow.

The Goddess rose. "The Chamber is only a room, though a magical one, and you will enter it when the time comes. Duke Roger is only a man, for all he wields sorcery. He can be met and defeated. But you, my daughter—learn to love. You have been given a hard road to walk. Love will ease it. Much depends on you, Alanna of Trebond. Do not fail me!"

Remembering her manners. Alanna jumped to her feet. "I won't fail you," she promised, her hand closing tight around the ember. "Or at least, I'll try not to."

"A goddess can ask no more." The Mother looked down at the little black animal sitting now by Alanna's feet. "Guard her well, Small One."

The kitten mewed in reply as Alanna glanced at him. Was there more to her new pet than she had thought?

The Goddess held out her hand. "Wear my token, and be brave. But remember—I did not jest when I said there are strange tales about this tree. Do not stray beyond your fire!" She smiled. "Fare well, my daughter."

Alanna kissed the immortal's hand, feeling weird energy jolt through her body. She stepped away, shaking her head to clear it. "Fare well, my Mother."

The Goddess walked over to Moonlight, caressing the mare for a moment and talking to her in a soft voice. Then she raised her hand to Alanna a last time, and she was gone.

Suddenly Alanna could barely keep her eyes open. It was a struggle to lay out her bedroll and to bank the fire, but she forced herself to perform the chores. Thinking about the strange conversation she had just had would have to wait. When she tumbled into her bedroll at last, the kitten was already inside.

"Don't snore," she ordered it sleepily. The kitten replied that he would not snore if she did not. Alanna nodded in agreement and went to sleep, tightly clutching the crystal ember.

～

It was a relief to get back to the palace the next day, back to familiar places and familiar friends. She still missed burly Coram, managing Trebond for her and Thom until she won her knight's shield, but there was no help for that. With Lord Alan dead and Thom not caring about anything but his studies, this arrangement was for the best, at least until Alanna was ready to begin adventuring. Then she would want Coram with her.

On her first night back she was feeding her new kitten his evening meal when she heard voices in Jonathan's room just before he knocked on her door.

"It's your overlord, Squire," Jonathan called. It was their private phrase that meant *There are people with me.* "Let me in!"

Alanna opened the connecting door, and Jonathan entered with their friends Gary and Raoul.

"We came to see if you wanted to go down to the Dancing Dove with us and visit George," Gary told her. "How about it?"

Alanna's face lit up. She hadn't had a long visit with the King of the Thieves since just before her father died, nearly six weeks ago. She was pulling on her boots when Raoul exclaimed, "Great Mithros, a cat! What are you doing with one of *those*? It probably has fleas."

Jonathan stopped to let the kitten sniff his fingers. "Can't you tell a sorcerer's familiar when you see one?" he joked. "And do familiars *have* fleas?" Picking the tiny animal up, he saw its face. His own sapphire-blue eyes widened. "Goddess!"

Raoul and Gary gathered around, staring at the kitten, whose eyes were the same color as their friend Alan's. Finally Raoul gulped and asked, "What will you name him? *Is* it a him?" Alanna nodded.

" 'Pounce,' " Jon suggested.

" 'Blackie,' " was Raoul's choice.

"How about 'Raoul'?" Gary wanted to know.

The kitten reached one paw for Alanna, mewing. She took her new pet from Jonathan and set him beneath her left ear—it was her favorite spot. "I rather like 'Faithful,'" she admitted.

Jonathan unsheathed his dagger. As if he were knighting the cat, he touched it on both shoulders, then on the head. "I dub thee 'Faithful,'" he said solemnly. "Serve honorably and well."

True to his name, Faithful followed Alanna everywhere. In the practice yards he claimed a convenient post where he could sit and watch her practice her fighting skills with the other squires and pages. It took him longer to sneak into most class-rooms. Myles let the kitten watch from the start, saying cats had the right to learn history as well as anyone. But Alanna's other teachers—most of them Mithran priests—tried to keep her pet out for days, but by the end of each class he had appeared inside. Finally the masters stopped trying. They even petted the cat absently as they taught.

There was one class Alanna refused to let Faithful come to: Duke Roger's class for those Gifted in magic (Alanna and Jonathan, among others). She didn't know what the sorcerer would think of her pet, and she didn't want to find out.

For the rest of the time, Faithful stuck to Alanna like a small black bur. Gareth, Duke of Naxen, Gary's father, let Faithful follow Alanna freely when he saw that the kitten took no one's attention away from learning. The sight of Alan with his pet under his left ear soon became a famil-iar one at the palace. While Faithful clearly liked Myles, Jon and most of Alanna's other friends (including George) and would stay with them when Alanna was busy, only she was given the priv-ilege of carrying him on a shoulder.

"Maybe he's afraid of heights," Gary suggested one rainy May afternoon, shortly after Alanna's fif-teenth birthday. It was a rare, quiet time for the young knights and Alanna. Gary and Raoul, with the afternoon off, had given their squires Geoffrey and Douglass free time as well. Raoul and Jonathan played backgammon, while Alex—the fifth member of their circle and the only one not secretly friends with George—watched. Gary sprawled in a window seat, thinking of a way to escape a visit to Naxen that summer. Alanna curled up in another window seat, listening to Faithful purr into her left ear and thinking about nothing at all.

"Hm?" Alanna asked sleepily, realizing Gary was talking to her.

"Faithful. Maybe he won't sit on our shoulders because he's afraid of heights."

"Maybe he's right." Jonathan grinned. "Even Alex is half a head taller than our Alan."

"Thanks," Alex said dryly.

The door opened, and Duke Roger came in. The family resemblance between him and Jonathan was unmistakable, although the Duke's eyes were a darker blue than his cousin's and his hair brown-black to Jon's coal-black. Both had the fair skin, straight-cut noses and stubborn chins that ran in the Conté line.

"There you are, Alex," the older man was saying. "I hate to ask this, but a truly important package has arrived for me at Port Caynn. You are the only one other than myself I trust to go. Will you?"

Alex grinned and stood. "It's my pleasure, Your—"

"Let go of me, you blasted cat!" Alanna yelped as Faithful's claws dug into her shoulder. His fur bristled; his back was arched; and he was growling deep in his throat as he stared at the Duke. Alanna tried to pry her pet loose as she said through gritted teeth, "Stop making a scene." The sorcerer was watching them!

His attention caught, the big man came forward. "A new pet, Alan?"

"He *was*, until he started *this*." Alanna worked Faithful loose and held him up. The kitten twisted to keep his eyes on Roger, growling. "What is the *matter* with you?" Alanna demanded, trying to make him look at her before Roger saw his eyes. "Behave yourself! Sir, he's never done this before—"

Roger drew a little closer, and Faithful slashed at him with unsheathed claws. "I think I'm being warned away," the sorcerer remarked, stopping where he was. He looked Faithful over as Alanna tried to work a large lump out of her throat. "Unusual eyes," he commented at last, and Faithful yowled. "I have just come from the kennels—perhaps he smells the dogs on me. Or perhaps he knows I have never been a fancier of—" He paused, and Alanna felt her skin turn to ice. "Of cats," he finished.

Alanna cradled her still-rumbling pet against her chest. Roger either knew or guessed where her pet came from, but he wasn't saying. That was fine with her. "It's probably the dogs, sir," she agreed. "He likes people and horses, but dogs don't suit him." the others looked at her, knowing as well as she did that Faithful left dogs alone, while dogs avoided Faithful. It wasn't *quite* a lie, and the Duke seemed to accept it. He nodded to Alex, and they left together.

When they were gone, Alanna picked the kitten up and read him an impressive lecture on manners. By the time she finished. Faithful was purring, her friends were laughing, and the whole thing had been forgotten—she hoped.

Nevertheless, that night she wrote her brother Thom in the City of the Gods, sending the letter secretly by way of George. Thom was the sorcerer—not she. He should know about Faithful—and about the cat's reaction to Duke Roger.

two

Duke Roger of Conté

*T*hat hot July an embassy came to court from Tortall's eastern neighbor, Tusaine. Important matters were to be discussed. Spies had reported the King of Tusaine was considering retaking the Drell River Valley on the Tortallan border, and King Roald wanted to avoid war at all costs. Unlike his famous father, Roald was not known as "Empire-Builder," but as "The Peacemaker." He was proud of that title, and he wanted to keep it. Everyone knew that Mikal of Danne, the Tusaine Ambassador, had actually come to see if "The Peacemaker" had the stomach for war.

The delegation from Tusaine was carefully watched, but its people received the best hospitality Roald could command. As Jonathan's squire, Alanna was very much in the thick of things, serving at secret meetings and accompanying her Prince to what seemed to be an endless number of parties and dances.

Tension was in the air. In the meetings, Ambassador Mikal became arrogant, thinking Roald was weak rather than quiet. Friendly discussions between Alanna's friends and the Tusaine knights grew sharp as each group challenged the other to more and more difficult contests of craft and skill. Matters finally came to a head during what was supposed to be a small, quiet evening party.

Alanna, Gary's squire, Sacherell of Wellam, and Raoul's squire, Douglass of Veldine, served the wine at this gathering, following Duke Gareth's instructions to keep their guests' glasses full and to report anything interesting they might overhear. Courtiers dressed in their finest chattered and flirted as the three obeyed with enthusiasm, trying to get as much from the Tusaine party as they could. Duke Roger entertained Mikal while the Ambassador's wife, Lady Aenne, told Queen Lianne and King Roald stories of the Tusaine Court.

Gary, Raoul, Alex and Jonathan were talking with some of the younger Tusaine knights, when suddenly everyone was looking at the group. Dain of Melor, a Tusaine knight, was sneering loudly, "Fencing! I've seen what *you* call 'fencing.' Back home we call it dancing! Prince Jonathan, our Tusaine *three*-year-olds handle a sword better than some of your knights!"

"You are rude in the palace of your host," Gary replied carefully, his broad shoulders tense. Alanna could tell he was fighting to keep his voice even. "I wish it were possible to teach you some manners."

For a moment no one spoke. Nearly every

Tortallan knight—with the exception of Myles, who was watching and drinking—had put his hand on his sword hilt. The Tusaines gripped theirs, ready for anything.

Ambassador Mikal turned to Roger. In the quiet his voice was very clear. "I must apologize for young Dain." He bowed in Roald's direction. The King inclined his head, silently accepting the apology. Mikal added with a sly smile, "I fear I must agree, however. We seem to have done better by the martial arts in Tusaine. Perhaps peace has dulled your fighting edge?"

Alanna touched the ember-stone beneath her shirt, wondering what would happen next. She turned. Raoul, standing by the hearth, was shifting slowly into a fighting stance. His coal-black eyes were snapping with fury, and he gripped his sword hilt with a white-knuckled hand.

Frantically she signaled Douglass to look at his knight-master. Her friend hurried over to Raoul and shoved a wineglass in the big knight's hand, talking softly and quickly. After a second's hesitation, Raoul released his hilt with a sigh.

"I differ with you, Sir Dain," Jon was saying, a touch of amusement in his voice. "Even our pages and squires know how to handle a sword against a full knight. But since our honor and our teachers are in question, perhaps we must show you what a Tortallan can do."

Dain adjusted his sword belt. "Bring on your

champion, Highness. I am sure I can prove Tusaine superiority over any man of your court."

Jon glanced at Alanna, smiling ironically, and she immediately guessed what he had in mind. *It would be a brilliant tactical stroke if I could pull it off,* she thought. *I'm an unblooded squire in Dain's eyes. At least, it would be a brilliant tactical stroke if I won.*

She looked the Tusaine knight over. He was a head taller than she was, with broad shoulders and strong arms, but he was overconfident, and he had been drinking. She nodded to let Jonathan know she was game.

The Prince smiled icily at the other man. "Not 'our champion,' Sir Dain. I said 'even our pages and squires.'" He nodded to Alanna. She handed her wine pitcher to Sacherell, who nearly dropped it, and walked quickly over to the group of young knights, her heart thumping with excitement. "Your Highness?" she asked, bowing politely.

Jonathan beckoned to her. "I'm sure my personal squire Alan here would oblige you."

The Tusaine knight stared at the short, slender Alanna, his jaw hanging open. "You want me to fence with a *squire?*" Dain's voice rose and cracked; someone giggled.

"Are you afraid?" Jonathan wanted to know.

The other man gasped and sputtered before he could speak again. "I've fought in six duels!" he snapped finally. "I've been killing mountain bandits since I was smaller than *him*." He pointed to Alanna. "If I was ever smaller than him!"

Alanna knew exactly what Jonathan was trying to do, and she knew it was her turn to add fuel to the fire. "Did you need me for something, my Lord Prince?"

Jonathan shrugged, his eyes never leaving Dain. "I thought you might fence with Sir Dain, Alan, but he no longer seems to be interested. I'm sorry to have called you away for nothing—"

"By Mithros, I'll do it!" Dain snapped. "I fear no child!"

Jonathan bowed to his parents. "If Your Majesties will excuse us, we would like to go to the first fencing gallery."

Turning to look at the King, Alanna saw the oddest look on Alex's face. He looked—eager, for some reason. Surely he wasn't looking forward to her risking her life? They had been friendly rivals for years—each trying to be better at fencing, archery and the other fighting skills than the other—but it was still *friendly* rivalry.

She forgot about Alex when she heard the king say, "I think this is something we will all want to see. Ambassador Mikal? Lady Aenne? My lady?"

The Queen and Lady Aenne nodded as Mikal said dryly, "It should be an interesting entertainment."

Servants were sent to prepare the largest of the indoor courts, while Duke Gareth's personal manservant, Timon, went to Alanna's quarters for Lightning. Everyone moved down to the court, Myles and Roger walking with the young men surrounding Alanna. Myles was upset and made no effort to pretend he wasn't.

"Are you going to throw away *everything?*" he demanded furiously. "He's a head taller than you are!"

Alanna shrugged. "Nearly everyone I fence with is." She accepted Lightning from Timon and buckled it on as Faithful yowled at her feet. Finally she picked the cat up and perched him on her shoulder. She had made the discovery that her pet's meowing actually sounded like talk to her, and she wanted to hear what he had to say now.

Let the foreigner be stupid, he advised. *It shouldn't be hard. And don't get yourself killed!*

"Are you *listening* to me?" Myles demanded. "This isn't the time to play hero!"

Jon rested a hand on Alanna's free shoulder. "Don't be so upset, Myles. Haven't you ever seen Alan fence? I have—in the Black City."

The memory of Alan's and Jon's strange adventure a year before—of the curse removed from the Black City and of thousands of proud Bazhir tribesmen kneeling in the streets of Persopolis—silenced Myles for a moment, but no longer.

"Dain is a practiced knight! It isn't the same!"

"Do you hear Father protesting?" Gary asked. "He's been teaching Alan and Alex privately for months now. Besides, you've got to trust Jonathan's judgment sometime. He doesn't try to get his friends killed."

Alex dropped back to talk with Duke Roger. "What do *you* think will happen?" the Duke asked his one-time squire.

A smile crossed Alex's dark, secret face. "I think Dain of Melor is in for a large surprise."

Roger shook his head, disbelieving. "Surely you don't mean to say Alan is as good as—well, you, for example."

"But I do. Alan's as good as I am. Someday he may be better."

Roger had no chance to pursue this further since they had arrived at the fencing gallery. Far below ground level, it was cool even in this hot weather. Torches in brackets on the walls threw light into all corners. Along one wall three rows of benches were set off from the main floor by a low rail. The courtiers sat down in a rustle of silks, Roger placing himself and Ambassador Mikal just behind the King and Queen.

At one end of the floor Dain was removing his boots and stretching himself, joking with his friends. On the other side a quiet Alanna watched Dain, ignoring her friends' talk. The Tusaine wasn't nervous—good for him. She would teach him how to be nervous.

Handing Faithful to Myles, she stripped off her own shoes and put on the tan fencing gloves Timon was holding for her. She didn't know that she was grinning recklessly, a merciless look in her violet eyes. Jonathan watched her thoughtfully. If he weren't so angry with Dain, he might feel sorry for the other knight. He knew what Alanna could do when she was forced to it.

Duke Gareth joined them. He bent down by Alanna as she began her stretching exercises. "Don't forget to let him tire himself out while you get his measure. I know the type. He'll try to make you angry with insults. Don't let that happen—keep your head. You're good, Alan, but you aren't the best."

Alanna grinned impishly up at him. "No, sir. You are."

The Duke of Naxen slapped her lightly on the shoulder. "Don't be pert. And *do* be careful."

Jonathan smiled. "Don't worry, Uncle. Alan keeps his head in a fight."

Mikal leaned toward Roger, not bothering to keep his voice low. "The squire is brave, but this is folly. Dain is good, very good. And he cannot always control his temper. I fear this evening will have a sorrowful ending."

Alanna and Dain stepped to the center of the floor, their unsheathed swords pointing down. Alanna fingered the ember-stone nervously under her shirt, wishing she felt calmer. The King stood.

"Are you prepared?"

They both faced him and bowed, then saluted

him with their swords. Quickly they bowed and saluted each other, then moved until they were just a sword's length apart.

"Cross your weapons," the King ordered. Alanna and Dain obeyed. "Do honor to the laws of chivalry and to the customs of your lands. Guard!"

Dain swung his blade around, meeting Alanna's with a clear, ringing sound. He bore down, trying to force her sword to the floor. Alanna gritted her teeth and held, the muscles in her arms screaming. Dain's eyes widened; she was much stronger than she looked. He broke away and circled her.

"Prepare to die, boy!"

Alanna did not reply. It was the custom to yell insults and challenges at an opponent, but she had always thought this was a waste of breath. She had also noticed that her unusual silence made her opponents nervous. Instead she watched Dain steadily, waiting for the movement of his torso that would give his next thrust away.

He whipped his sword down and in. Alanna struck it away and slid her own blade straight toward Dain's heart, ready to pull back if she had to. Dain stepped back hurriedly, and Alanna lunged back before she went off-balance.

"A child's trick!" Dain scoffed.

The King winked back at Roger. "That 'child's trick' nearly worked," he murmured, to Ambassador Mikal's obvious discomfort.

Dain was circling and talking, trying to keep

Alanna distracted until he spotted her weakness. He lunged in and back with great speed, searching for her one failure to fend him off. Alanna parried his blows and watched for an opening she would use to knock the sword from his hand: she wanted no bloodshed. Sweat was trickling down her cheeks, making her nervous—what if it got in her eyes? It was no comfort that Dain's shirt and tunic were soaked through on the chest and between his shoulder blades, or that he was breathing in deep, heavy gasps. Alanna grinned to herself. *He should have begun fencing with Coram's big old sword,* she thought. *Then he wouldn't be so tired now.*

Frantic, Dain insulted her ancestors, her mother, her looks. Alanna ignored him, far more worried about the sweat she could feel on her forehead. The only sound in the big room was the padding of their stockinged feet and Dain's harsh breathing. Alanna spotted a chance and lunged desperately—Dain stumbled back. She tried to wipe her face on her sleeve while he recovered.

She wasn't quick enough. With a yell of triumph the knight darted forward. She stepped back too slowly, and the tip of Dain's sword sank deep into her right arm below the elbow. Cursing her bad timing, Alanna lowered her blade. She had lost. According to the rules, Dain had won by drawing first blood. The fight was over.

He lunged for her chest, his eyes wide and crazy. Alanna jumped aside, just missing dying on the Tusaine's sword.

"Foul!" Gary yelled, furious. Others joined him, yelling "Foul!"

Dain ignored them. He circled Alanna, searching for another opening. Duke Gareth strode forward, his sword shimmering in his fist. He obviously planned to end the fight, and from the look on his face, if Dain got hurt it would be too bad for him!

Alanna stopped her teacher with a shake of the head. A cold, glittering fury filled her chest. She loved the laws of chivalry, and this Tusaine barbarian had just broken them. He would pay for that, and pay well.

Slowly she stepped back and away from Dain, painfully transferring Lightning into her left hand. Blood dripped onto the floor from her right arm. *I'll have to be careful and not slip in it,* she thought as she readied herself.

Faithful yowled encouragement as Alanna lunged forward viciously. Lightning met Dain's sword with a crash. Instantly she pulled away, then thrust in again. The knight blocked clumsily, falling back as she bore in on him. Her sword never stopped moving; she never stopped looking for an opening. There it was!

She brought Lightning down, under and up, catching Dain's hilt and yanking the sword from his hand. It went flying. In his haste to escape, the man stumbled, falling flat. Alanna darted forward to press Lightning's brightly gleaming point into

Dain's throat. The Tusaine knight looked up into the coldest eyes he ever hoped to see.

"Stupid," Alanna told him quietly, her voice shaking with fury. "That was very stupid. And you're lucky I'm a better 'knight' than you are, or you'd be dead." She turned contemptuously and walked back to her friends, letting Jon brace her as Duke Gareth bound up her wound.

"He was holding back," Ambassador Mikal murmured thoughtfully. "All along—that boy was holding back." He looked at Roald. "If all your young knights are like that one squire, your army must be formidable indeed."

"See for yourself." The King pointed to Jonathan, quiet and commanding; big Gary and even bigger Raoul; slender, dark Alex with his cat-like grace. "They are part of our future," the King said. "It is a future we all want to protect."

∼

*A*lanna was cleaning Lightning in her room when Myles found her. "You didn't kill him," the knight said bluntly. "He would have killed you, but you didn't kill him."

Alanna's arm was hurting; she hadn't yet gotten the chance to place healing magic on herself. The pain made her short with her friend. "So? He was stupid. If I killed everyone who was stupid, I wouldn't have time to sleep."

"He gave you every excuse to kill him," Myles

persisted. "Even his Ambassador would have under-stood if you had."

"Just because *he* behaved badly is no excuse for *me* to behave badly." Alanna's lower lip began to tremble. It was too much excitement. She wanted to go to bed, and she wanted to heal her arm so it would stop throbbing. "Why are you picking on me? You of all people should've known I wouldn't kill him."

Myles hugged her tightly, taking care not to bump her wounded arm. "You're a good lad, Alan of Trebond," he whispered. "You give an old man hope."

"Nonsense," Alanna growled, pleased and embarrassed by the unexpected praise. "You aren't that old. And I'm not that good a lad."

～

Duke Roger settled into the chair before his fire, picking up a chess piece from the game set up there. It was a pawn. The man smiled ironically; before the Black City he had thought Alan of Trebond was a pawn. A Gifted, athletic pawn, but a pawn nevertheless; a pawn who could be moved around by Roger. The Black City—and tonight's bout with Dain—had taught him differently. Alan of Trebond was dangerous.

Jonathan should not have returned from the Black City. Roger knew that place of evil well, and he knew the Ysandir who lived there were invincible. That was why he had taken the risk, using magical suggestion to make Jonathan need to visit the forbidden place. But Jonathan had taken Alan with him, and both had come back alive. Two young, untried boys had not only escaped the Ysandir, they had destroyed them!

Roger made a face and poured himself some wine. At least one of the gods was protecting Jonathan, maybe more; he was certain of that. It did not matter; if he had to throw earth and the heavens into chaos to get the Tortallan throne, he would.

Alan of Trebond! What did he know about the lad? What powers did the boy have?

Pacing his chamber furiously now, the sorcerer remembered the Sweating Sickness. He had brewed a fever that would drain any healer who pursued it, sending it to both city and palace in order to make sure every healer in the capital would be too weak to help when the Prince fell ill. But Jonathan had survived, and the healer-lad with the wide purple eyes told Roger that Sir Myles had shown him what to do. Myles was a scholar: it was possible he had read spells that could counteract even powerful magic.

So he, Roger, had accepted Alan's story. Then he had questioned the boy further, reaching into his mind to see if Alan had any secrets. He remembered that moment even now—feeling his magic sliding over glass walls behind those innocent eyes.

If he had touched a power that attacked him, he might have probed the boy with *real* sorcery. Instead he thought the slipperiness was stupidity or thoughtlessness. He had let the page go without looking further. Three times more a fool!

There was the sword, the battered and ancient sword that Myles "just happened" to have in his armory: Roger's arm had been numb for a week after touching it. And the cat! If Faithful was an ordinary cat, Roger would swallow his wizard's rod whole. So far it seemed Alan didn't know the value of his weapons, but his "ignorance" had fooled Roger before. Even if he did not know their uses now, he would surely learn them in the future.

And tonight Alan had revealed another important quality he could bring to Jonathan's service: he had shown he was a great swordsman, one who could fight as well—if not better—with his left hand as with his right. Roger swore again and gulped down another glass of wine. Why had Alex never told him? Jealousy? A refusal to believe a boy who was still a squire could be as good as he was?

The Duke scowled, fingering his short beard. He would have to be more careful now than ever; Alan, he felt, suspected him, and Alan must never get proof to back up his suspicions. Of course, there were ways and ways to handle that aspect of things. Some steps might be taken soon.

More important, Roger needed to get rid of Alan in some way that appeared natural. In fact, it might be impossible to dispose of Jonathan without first killing Alan. But it would have to be handled carefully, subtly. He could not rouse anyone's suspicions.

Roger did not want a violent civil war that would leave Tortall ruined and poor. He wanted no enemies like Duke Gareth or Sir Myles. He only wanted his uncle, his aunt and his cousin to die natural-seeming deaths within the next five years, so no one could claim he had stolen his throne. He was in no hurry. He could afford to wait, now that the Queen could have no more children; although it would do no harm to ensure that Duke Gareth, Myles and perhaps even the King never looked at him with suspicion.

And Alan of Trebond, who already suspected? That needed study. He must certainly put his mind to the problem of Alan of Trebond.

three

The Prince's Squire

*L*ate one night in August—the night before Jonathan's birthday—Alanna made for the Dancing Dove, the inn that served as a meeting place for the Court of the Rogue. Reminding Faithful to behave himself, she settled the cat firmly on her shoulder and entered the inn. It took a moment for her to adjust to the smoke and noise in the large common room; the thieves and their women were louder than usual. They greeted Alanna and Faithful with yells of approval, inviting squire and cat to join them.

Alanna nodded to George, the Rogue himself, who was sitting at his usual place beside the now-empty hearth. "Thanks," she told the others, "but I'm here on an errand."

"Are ye ever here t' drink?" Scholar wanted to know. "What a sober youngling! Ye an' Johnny!" (None of the thieves knew George's friend, the rich young Johnny, was in truth Prince Jonathan.) "Ye never have a drop!"

"'Tis unnatural!" Lightfingers bellowed. He yanked a pretty flower-seller called Laughing Nell onto his lap. "Alan, ye won't even have a drink t' celebrate th' Prince's birthday?"

Alanna grinned. "You're celebrating His Highness's birthday? It's not even midnight! Does he know you're so loyal, 'Fingers?"

George stood, commanding everyone's attention. "Lightfingers just likes to drink, Alan." 'Fingers nodded and grinned. "And if he can't find an excuse, he drinks from sorrow. Come upstairs, lad."

Alanna followed the King of the Thieves to his chambers, sinking into a chair with relief. "Goddess, I'm tired!" she said with a yawn as Faithful let George scratch his ears. "Up before dawn today, and again tomorrow. Maybe I should change my mind and become a stableboy or something."

George poured them each a glass of wine, then threw open the shutters, letting the cool night breeze rush in. "Anyone who wishes to be a knight is mad, to my way of thinkin'. I hear you did well in your lessons with Duke Gareth today."

Alanna laughed as Faithful explored the room. "George, you amaze me. I wish the King's spies in Tusaine were as good as you are."

"That can be arranged," the thief murmured.

Alanna sat bolt upright. "You mean you could—you would—"

"I think I could be makin' some inquiries, yes. But *you* had best be certain you find a way of concealin' your source."

"Yes, that *would* be a problem." Alanna nodded.

"I'll think about that part of it, then, and you— would you make your inquiries?" She smiled at him shyly. "It could be important. You know what the situation is with Tusaine."

George unlocked a large chest in the corner of the room, lifting out a bulky package and a small one and putting them on the table. "Of course," he said. "I wouldn't do it for the King, but for you and Jon I will. Aren't we friends? Here, lass. From Lord Thom in the City of the Gods to yours truly to you."

The large package contained a silver chain mail shirt decorated with tiny diamonds and sapphires and a belt of woven silver wire. Glowing with pleasure, for Alanna had rarely seen such beautiful work, she opened her twin's letter.

Sister Dear,
I trust this will serve adequately as Trebond's honorarium on the occasion of His Highness's birthday. Are you trying to break my treasury? Just don't forget to mention my name. I did as you asked and put some protective spells on the shirt and belt. In fact, I put the strongest on them I could find. The Masters questioned us for days, trying to find out who used so much magic without permission. I knew you would want the best.
Once again questions about us are being asked in the City. I think at least one of the

new servants hired here at the Mithran Cloisters is also being paid to keep an eye on me. So I play twice as stupid, and I'm being very careful. Perhaps you'll say I worry too much, but I believe you did something to make your "smiling friend" nervous. Think about it. Give my regards to the dishonorable George, and of course formal regards from the Lord of Trebond to the Royal Family—you know how to handle that sort of thing.

Thom.

Alanna read the letter to George before burning it in the candleflame. "He's got delusions," she said flatly. "Why would Duke Roger take special interest in us *now?*"

George swallowed his drink and poured another. "Weren't you tellin' me the Duke's been testin' your magic a bit lately? And twice you've been followed into the city by palace men."

Alanna stared at the thief. "*Followed?*"

George patted her shoulder. "They never got so far as the marketplace. I always have you or the lads watched on your way here by my people, in case my Lord Provost decides there's oddness in your city visits."

Alanna frowned. "Why follow me, or have Thom watched? And why *has* he been testing my magic?"

George shrugged broad shoulders. "This is

dated July, and you beat Dain of Melor in June. He started testin' your magic after the Black City; that was a year ago. Your bein' followed dates from June, too. I'd say you worried him with your magic last year, and with your strength at arms when you beat Dain."

Alanna sighed and shook her head. "That doesn't make sense."

George smiled thinly. "Ah, but it does, and you well know it."

Alanna knew what he meant, and she didn't want to even think about it. She changed the subject. "Anyway, thanks. Listen, I'll keep my ears peeled around my Lord Provost. You've been more than a friend. I don't want anything to happen to you."

George smiled at her. "With friends like you and Jon, I doubt much ever will." Suddenly his face was very thoughtful. "How old are you, lass?"

Alanna smiled at him. "You ought to know, I just turned fifteen."

He took one of her hands in his two large ones. "We marry as young as fifteen here in the city."

Alanna laughed. "I'm not going to marry, George, you know that."

"Shouldn't you know what love's like before you begin renouncin' it?" George was watching her, the oddest look in his eyes. Alanna's heart beat too fast; her hand was still in his. He stood, pulling her to her feet close to him.

"George, you've been celebrating too much." She tried to keep her voice light and relaxed. "I never thought I'd hear you talk like this."

"Why not?" His voice was as relaxed and careless as hers. If only he would let go of her hand!

"Because—well, because you know me better. I have other plans."

"You're not even curious?" He refused to look away. She had never noticed before how much green was in his hazel eyes, or how long his lashes were.

She *had* to pull her hand away, even if it was rude. "No," she said flatly. This conversation was far too personal! "I'm not curious at all."

Faithful, who had been sleeping on the windowsill, yawned and stretched.

"Quite right," Alanna told her cat. Nervously she gathered up the package containing the shirt and belt. "I've got to go," she announced.

He gathered up his sword belt. "I'll just go with you as far as the Temple District. You're carryin' valuables, remember, and even *I* don't trust my folk completely. Good swordsman you are, but you might be outnumbered." He grinned as he fastened the belt around his hard waist. "Besides, one of your attackers may be a wrestler."

Alanna made a face at him, relieved he was talking sensibly once more. "Thanks, I *love* having my nose rubbed in my weakness."

George tucked the second, unopened package

into his shirt front. "You'd worry me if you didn't have *some* weaknesses, little one," he informed her. "We'll take the back stairs."

It was fun to walk through the Lower City with him, talking about the upcoming celebrations while Faithful dashed off after real or imaginary prey. It was so late that no one was out to see them. Her hands *were* full with Jon's gift, and she knew anyone would think twice about attacking a man who moved with such muscular grace. Also, sometimes it was pleasant just to *be* with George, to relax and to forget about being a noble, about the Ordeal, about being a girl fighting to win a knight's shield. George just let her be who she was.

"Hm?" she asked, realizing his last remark had been a question.

"I said, are things with the Tusaine nobles so serious? The rogues in Tusaine think it's all just a court storm, but they admit they don't know their nobles as well as we." George's teeth flashed in a grin.

"Serious enough, I think," she admitted. "Anything you learn will help."

"Then I'll do my best." They had reached the edge of the Temple District. George could leave her there safely: the District was patrolled by warriors of different faiths, and the rest of the Palace Way was in full view of the Royal Guard.

The thief pulled her into the shade of a large tree, where they couldn't be seen by anyone passing by, and drew the small package out of his shirt front. "This is from me to Jon. Be sure you give it to him in private. You don't want folk askin' questions about the giver."

Alanna tucked the gift into the large bundle, juggling it all with difficulty. She looked up at her friend accusingly. "George, did you—"

He laughed merrily. "Oh, you mistrustin' child! No, I did *not* steal it. I had it made special for Jon. It's quite pretty, even if I did have to pay for it myself." He looked around, checking to see if anyone was coming, then suddenly tilted her face up with one hand. "Alanna," he whispered, "I'm takin' advantage of you now, because I may never catch you with your hands full again." He kissed her softly and carefully. Alanna trembled, too shocked to do anything but let it happen.

"There." George released her. "Think over what I said about love."

"Pigs might fly," she snapped, her voice shaking. "I should have stabbed you!"

He chuckled infuriatingly. "No. I won't let you stab me and ruin our friendship. Will you be afraid to face me again after this?"

Alanna felt herself turning beet red. This was too much! "I'm afraid of no one, George Cooper," she yelled. "Especially not you!"

"Until next time, then." He saluted her and headed back down to the city, whistling. Faithful rubbed against Alanna's ankles, purring.

"Where were you when I needed you?" she asked him bitterly. "As a chaperone you aren't much."

I'm not here as a chaperone, the cat replied. *Besides, I didn't want to interrupt. You seemed to be enjoying yourself.*

There was no way of replying to such obvious silliness. Alanna turned and walked quickly—*very* quickly—back to the palace.

∽

*A*lthough Alanna later remembered very little of the daylight celebrations in honor of Jonathan's nineteenth birthday, she remembered the ball that night vividly. That was when she met Delia of Eldorne for the first time.

She had been sitting in a window seat, bored and miserable, when Gary found her. She hated parties, and normally the only way she attended one was when she was pouring drinks and serving food as a squire. Tonight, however, servants waited on the guests, and as Jonathan's squire she had been practically *ordered* to attend. She considered it a useless exercise. She couldn't converse with strangers easily, and she certainly couldn't flirt with the ladies as her friends did! She was busy calculating an escape when Gary, magnificent in brown velvet, discovered her hiding place. "I know you hate social events, but you'll never get used to them this way."

"I don't have to get used to them," Alanna retorted. "If I get my shield, I'm riding off on adventures."

"Nonsense!" Her friend grinned. "Come out of your shell. There are plenty of noblewomen who'd like to meet the Prince's squire, especially since June."

"I'm only fifteen," Alanna replied automatically. "I'm too young for girls."

Gary smoothed his new mustache. "You're never too young for girls. Come on. I'll introduce you to the newest arrival. She just came yesterday, and *Mithros!*" He whistled his approval, adding smugly, "I got to meet her first." He clamped a hand around Alanna's arm and levered her out of her seat, walking her out onto the floor. It was either walk or be dragged; Alanna sometimes wondered if Gary knew his own strength.

She saw the trouble spot immediately: Jonathan stood at the center of a cluster of knights. He was talking to someone hidden from Alanna's view. The young men moved out of Gary's way, spotting Alanna and grinning. Squire Alan's reluctance to meet young ladies was palace legend.

Jonathan saw them and smiled, beckoning them forward. "Gary, you found him. Alan, come here."

A royal command was a royal command. Alanna moved up to stand beside the Prince, but she wasn't happy about it.

Seated at the center of the cluster of men was a lovely girl with chestnut-colored hair. Alanna lifted an eyebrow. Most maidens at Court wore pale colors or whites, but this one was wearing a low-cut green silk dress. Well, the color *did* emphasize her bright-green eyes as a lighter color would not.

Jonathan was bowing to the vision. "Lady Delia of Eldorne, I'd like you to meet my personal squire, Alan of Trebond."

Alanna bowed and found herself presented with a dainty white hand. Blushing slightly, she brushed it with her lips. Never was she more aware of her real sex than at moments like these! She looked up into Delia's face, noting the pert little nose and full red lips. *She's a beauty, all right,* Alanna realized. *And she knows it.*

"Alan of Trebond," Delia murmured, her voice light and throaty. "I've heard of you, haven't I?" She tapped her rosy mouth with her fan, delicate dark brow carefully arched. Then she laughed merrily. "The 'Squire's squire!' And you beat that dreadful knight from Tusaine. I think that's thrilling!"

Alanna bowed politely. "It was nothing, Lady Delia," she murmured.

"Oh, but you're being modest. I'm sure no Tortallan thinks it was 'nothing'—do you, gentlemen?" Delia asked the bristlingly jealous knights around her. Alanna knew very well that at the moment her friends were wishing *they* had beaten Dain, and that *she* was far, far away. In that Alanna was one with them. She didn't like Delia, and she wanted to leave. "Do you dance, Alan of Trebond?" Delia asked now.

Jonathan, grinning wickedly, replied, "Of course he knows how to dance. He learned the steps as a page, as did we all." Alanna promptly resolved to put something soft and squishy in her friend's bed—very soon.

"And he was always stepping on someone's feet," Raoul muttered.

Delia placed her hand on Alanna's arm, rising gracefully from her chair. "I'm sure he dances beautifully now." She laughed.

The Code of Chivalry was very specific about moments like this. Red as a beet, Alanna led Delia out onto the dance floor as the musicians struck up a waltz. She had never felt so ridiculous in her life. Delia was even taller than she was!

Carefully Alanna whirled Delia around the floor as the girl chattered about how kind everyone was, particularly Prince Jonathan. She knew now she didn't like Delia at all, and she felt very odd whenever Delia complimented Jonathan. Finally it was over, and she returned the young noblewoman to her admirers. Good manners or no, she was going. Even the Chamber of the Ordeal had to be better than dancing with a green-eyed flirt.

She bumped into Myles on her way out. Her friend was worse for wear, to put it mildly.

He toasted her with his glass of brandy. "Not

sociable, Alan?" Myles asked. "You'd better learn to be. A knight is a social animal."

"I'd sooner kiss a—"

"Don't, please. Sometimes you're too frank for an old man."

Alanna looked him over. "Need help getting back to your rooms?" she asked.

"No. I'm staying to watch the pretty little Eldorne girl try to hook every eligible male at Court."

Alanna clenched her jaw. "If she doesn't succeed, it won't be because she didn't try."

Myles lifted both eyebrows. "Jealous about Jonathan?"

"Why should I be jealous about Jonathan?" she snapped.

Myles shrugged. "Some women like to break up men's friendships. If I were you, I'd keep that in mind."

"I'll stop by in the morning with my hangover remedy. It sounds as if you'll need it." Sometimes the odd things Myles told her made too much sense for her peace of mind.

"You're a good human being, Alan. Too good to be caught up in Court games. Run along to bed."

Alanna obeyed, thinking. By "Court games" Myles meant the tricks peopled used to win favor with important nobles, to get revenge on each other or to acquire power. Was that the kind of game Delia played? Whatever it was, it left a sour taste in Alanna's mouth.

∾

*I*t was a hard winter for Alanna, and she sometimes wondered if she spent all of it in a bad temper. The cold was worse than she could ever
remember, biting into her bones at every turn. Too
often she awoke shivering in the night, despite
Faithful, plenty of hot bricks and a well-banked
fire. Once or twice she caught herself wondering
what would happen if she climbed in with
Jonathan! When the cold got that bad, she used her
Gift to warm herself. The effort left her tired and
cross in the morning, but to Alanna *anything* was
better than feeling cold and thinking such
thoughts. On days when she worked in the outdoor
practice courts, she remembered the heat of the
Great Southern Desert with longing.

The temperatures meant trouble at home, as
well. Coram wrote her that early frosts had hurt the
harvest, and Alanna found herself busy arranging
for food and warm clothing to be sent to Trebond.
Coram was doing his best, but he had not had a
great deal of time to bring the fief back from Lord
Alan's neglect. More than once Alanna went to
Myles and Duke Gareth for advice. *For someone
who's never going to run a fief,* she often thought
wryly, *I'm certainly getting plenty of practice.*

That winter, as a preliminary test to prepare the
squires for the Ordeal, they were required to spend
a January night out in the open in the Royal Forest.
Biting back an unreasoning feeling of terror—she

would *not* freeze to death, if she took care—Alanna readied the things she would need. Out on her own, she burrowed deep into a snowbank and made a snug little cave for her tent and her fur-lined bedroll. A tree behind would keep off the worst of the drifts if more snow should fall. Faithful chose to keep her company, and he seemed much warmer than she felt (even though she wore fleece-lined leather over several layers of wool and silk clothing).

She had planned to go ice-fishing for her dinner, just to show Duke Gareth she *could* survive in the cold; but late in the afternoon a sudden blizzard rolled in, dousing the woods in the snow. Alanna and Faithful secured themselves in their burrow, and from time to time Alanna thrust Lightning through into the air to keep them from suffocating. For the rest of the night she and the cat slept—and talked. She knew it sounded like meowing to most other people, but to her Faithful talked as understandably as any human.

They had both fallen asleep toward dawn, when the blizzard's howling winds finally stopped. Alanna was dreaming of the desert and of a warm nap in he sun when she came wide awake. Something grunting and determined was digging in the snow overhead. Faithful's violet eyes glowed in the darkness beside her.

"I think it's a boar," Alanna hissed as soundless as she could. "It figures." Carefully, moving as little as possible, she worked Lightning up and free. When an ugly, cloven hoof burst through the beaten snow over the tent opening, Alanna thrust upward with all her strength. She burst from the snow, shaking clumps from her face, to feel her sword wrenched from her hand.

The boar was squealing with rage, trying to dislodge the blade that was driven through his chest and back. Suddenly he stiffened and fell. Alanna walked toward him carefully, seeing a glaze coming over his eyes. Gripping her swordhilt to pull it free, she stopped; the boar's eyes were a demonic red. Suddenly he shuddered one last time—and vanished.

Wordlessly Alanna gathered up her things. She didn't need Faithful to tell her—as he was, forcefully—that someone had just tried to kill her: someone with a command of sorcery. "I have no proof," she snapped, and that was the end of it. She would never tell anyone until she had proof.

On top of everything else, there was Delia. More than once that winter Alanna thought that if she heard the lovely girl's name once more, she would scream. Jonathan spent his free time writing bad poetry to Delia and insisting that Alanna listen to him read it. Gary and Raoul fought a duel over one of her riding gloves, and Duke Gareth sent them both on border patrols to cool off. The only good thing about this punishment was that they had to take Douglass and Sacherell with them;

even those two had been bitten by romance.

Alanna continued to dislike the girl unreasonably, staying away from her as much as she could. She sometimes felt that Delia knew Alanna detested her. She also thought Delia liked to have Jonathan's squire giving her special service: fanning Delia when she was hot, bringing her glasses of lemonade, even dancing with her; all activities that got Alanna into trouble with her lovesick friends. Jonathan went so far as to accuse her of using Delia to make her masquerade as a boy seem more believable! He later apologized, but it was their first big fight, and Alanna couldn't quite forgive Delia for being the cause.

Alanna was forced to listen when Jon ranted about Delia's flirtations with other knights, and she suffered through his attempts at poetry. She tried to be the best friend to him she could, because it was obvious (to her, if not to Jonathan) that Delia was toying with him. The girl would convince Jon one day that she was his alone, and ignore him the next. Soon they were sleeping together—sometimes. Which only made it worse. Jon was cross and elated by turns.

Only Alex and his squire, Geoffrey of Meron, seemed unaffected by Delia, and it was a welcome change to talk with them. It was during one such conversation with Alex on a windy day in March that Alanna discovered they wanted to test each other. Before he had passed the Ordeal, Alex had been the best of the squires; now he was getting a reputation as one of the finest knights in Tortall.

He and Alanna had been talking about what it was like to be good, with everyone watching for mistakes, until it was only natural to find one of the indoor fencing courts and see which of them was better. They had agreed a referee was not necessary, since they were only using blunt practice swords. Not even Faithful was there.

Alanna watched Alex stretch as she did so herself, excitement running through her veins. She had always wondered if she was as good as her dark friend. Now she would find out.

Their stretching finished, they saluted each other with the practice swords. Without warning Alex struck, his hand flashing in a complex overhand pass that brought his blade within inches of Alanna's unguarded face. Only a quick backward leap saved her. She circled, watching Alex's chest. With all but the best fighters, muscle movements in the chest often betrayed the direction of the next attack—except Alex was one of the best. Like Duke Gareth, who fought without signals, Alex moved without warning. He swept his sword up and under; the blow would have ripped Alanna open from abdomen to chest if they had been using real swords. She lunged back once more, but not quickly enough. The tip of Alex's sword sliced up her thigh, tearing her hose and gouging a deep scratch in her leg.

"Hey, Alex!" she protested. "Be careful!"

The knight did not answer. His dark face was emotionless, his eyes unreadable. Alanna faded back, then lunged to the side and the front, coming at him in a straightforward strike. Alex met her: their swordhilts locked. Body-to-body, Duke Gareth called it, and it rarely happened. For someone as small as Alanna it meant real trouble. Alex strained, forcing his weight down, trying to make her fall to her knees. Alanna broke away and came back instantly, knocking his blade aside. The flat of her sword struck Alex hard on the cheekbone, and she stepped back, feeling ashamed. It was disgraceful to let her temper get away with her as she just had.

"Alex, I'm sorry," she said ruefully, looking at the welt spreading across his dark skin. "Do you—"

Alex brought up his sword again, smiling slightly. His dark eyes glittered with something she couldn't name. He whispered, "Guard."

Alanna was suddenly tired of this game. Determined to end the match one way or another, she lunged in. Alex locked with her again and knocked her to the floor.

Alanna rolled. Alex's sword-point struck the floor an inch away from her head, taking a chip out of the hard wood. She glimpsed his face, and what she saw frightened her. His eyes were bright; the smile on his lips was suddenly nasty. She jumped up as he came at her again, but she wasn't quick enough. The flat of his blade smacked against her ribs, making her gasp for air. She swung at his side and connected hard, making him wince with pain.

This time she put her sword down. "I want to stop," she told him. "Something's wrong!"

She got her sword up just in time as he struck. Their blades met and sparks flew. Alanna disengaged and got away.

Sweat trickled into her eyes; she shook her head to clear them. This was insane! He acted as if he really wanted to kill her; with a dull practice sword death would be *very* painful.

Alex closed in, unstoppable. He brought his sword up and over his head, coming down hard. Alanna dodged aside just in time; the blunt edge struck her collarbone rather than her skull. Bone cracked in her shoulder as she fell to her knees with a cry of pain. Helplessly she watched the sword swing up and down, unable to stop its slicing toward her throat. She closed her eyes. If he hit her in the neck, he would break it, and there was nothing she could do.

"Very interesting, Alex."

Miraculously, Alex dropped his blade and turned. Myles stood just inside the door, Faithful at his feet. "You've certainly proved you're better than Alan. Of course, you *are* four years older, and you have several battles to your credit." The older knight's words whipped through the air like a lash. "However, I think you two have played 'Best

Warrior' long enough. Or didn't you realize you had injured Alan?"

Alex turned to Alanna. The nasty smile was replaced by concern. "Alan, I didn't—here, let me help you up—"

"Don't touch me!" Alanna cried as he reached for her. She quickly added, "Please, Alex—it's my collarbone. I think it's broken."

Alex knelt beside her, his face tense. "Alan, I'll never forgive myself—"

She smiled tightly, beginning to feel sick. "It's all right. We just got a little carried away. With my Gift I'll be fine in a couple of days."

Alex looked at Myles. "Sir Myles, I didn't—"

"The Provost is looking for you," Myles replied, his sharp eyes never leaving Alex's face. "I believe he has a border patrol ready. It must have been hard on you, cooped up this winter while everyone else got duties."

Alex stood. "If there's anything I can do—"

Alanna nodded, sweat standing out on her forehead. "I'll let you know right away."

Alex hurried out, and Myles crossed to Alanna. "Just lie still," he told her. "I'll get a healer—and some servants. We'll have to carry you out, I'm afraid."

"What brought you here?" Alanna whispered. "No one knew..."

Myles nodded to the cat bumping Alanna's good hand. "Faithful brought me. He was very forceful! I'm glad I listened. Alan, Alex was trying to kill you."

Alanna shook her head, the effort bringing on a wave of nausea. "He's been my friend for years."

He didn't look so very friendly when we walked in, Faithful told her.

Alanna grimaced. "I don't want to hear any more about it." But in her mind a voice was saying, *He hasn't been a close friend in years—not since he became Duke Roger's squire.* She sighed and put the thought away to go over later, when her head wasn't spinning. Until she had proof, she had to keep her suspicions to herself.

four

A Cry of War

The April rains poured down outside the Dancing Dove as Alanna examined the scrap of dirty paper George had given her, wishing it would go away. "There's no chance of a mistake?" she asked her friend.

"None," the thief replied. "I've received the same reports from the castles where the troops are hid and from the Rogue in Tusaine's capital. Duke Hilam, King Ain's brother, sees himself as a conqueror. He's mobilized all their armies, and the spearhead points right at the Drell River. With the mountain passes open…" He shrugged. "I give it two more weeks before they're locked onto the river's right bank. The fort there won't hold out much more than a week once Duke Hilam attacks."

Alanna looked at the tiny map. "What a stupid place to fight a war," she whispered. "It's enclosed by mountains. Neither side will have room to turn. The mountains will slow down reinforcements, supplies. And we're going to be doing a lot of fighting in the river." She folded the map up and stuck it in her shirt. "Thanks, George."

"I just wish I had good news." The thief's fingers touched her chin gently, making her look up. Alanna blushed. He hadn't kissed her since Jon's birthday almost a year ago; but he let her know—with little touches, with softness in his eyes when he looked at her—that he was stalking her. Jonathan looked at Delia in much the same way. That Alanna got such attention from George terrified her.

"I have to leave," she said, gathering up her cloak.

"All right, then." He opened the door for her. "Let me know what's done."

Alanna couldn't help but grin. "Don't be silly. You'll probably know before me." She hurried out into the rainy night.

She found Myles of Olau in his chambers, translating some ancient document. Faithful was curled up before the knight's fire, having told Alanna he preferred napping before a warm hearth to trotting to the City in the rain. He greeted Alanna now by leaping onto her shoulder.

The moment Myles saw her face he put his translating aside. "What's wrong?"

Alanna pulled the folded map from beneath her shirt, watching Myles's face as she opened it. "You have some friends in the City," she replied softly. "A young burglar named Marek. An old man who forges called Scholar." She smiled. "They say you're a good drinking companion. I could've told them that." Myles opened his mouth to speak, but Alanna shook her head. "I'm not asking you to admit anything. I'm telling you I know Marek and Scholar and their friends. I'm friends with the man who rules them."

"The Rogue himself?" Myles whispered. "How?"

"It's too long a story, but I've known him and the others for years. Last summer I told George— the Rogue—that we were having trouble getting good information from Tusaine. He offered to help." Alanna handed the map to her friend. "He gave me this today. The little red arrows are Tusaine legions—"

Myles counted them. "Twenty." He whistled. "At one hundred men per legion—two thousand foot soldiers."

"The blue arrows are units, ten armed knights each."

"One hundred and fifty in all." Myles looked at the map, rubbing his forehead wearily. "They're quartered in these castles and towns?"

Alanna nodded. "And look what they're circled around."

"The Drell River Valley." Myles looked at Alanna. "How much do you trust the Rogue?"

"I trust him with my life. I trust him with Jon's life."

Myles rose. "Duke Gareth and the King must see this immediately. I'll be certain your name and that of your source don't come into the discussion.

"One more thing, Myles. George says the mountain passes from Tusaine into the Drell Valley are open."

"Then we've very little time, and we're not prepared." Myles shook his shaggy head. "Gareth and I tried to convince Roald that Hilam would do this. If we were dealing only with King Ain, there'd be no trouble. He just wants to be left in his pleasure gardens with his wives. But Hilam—"

"Has notions?" Alanna suggested.

∾

*M*yles's information had an immediate effect on the palace. Every high-ranking nobleman was summoned to the War Chamber to confer all the next day and late into the night. Messengers and carrier pigeons went out from the castle in droves as the halls buzzed with gossip. Alanna could only wait. Jonathan was included in the discussions, but his squire was not.

She was reading in her rooms late the next night when the Prince returned at last. He shook his head when she gestured toward a chair. "I'm for bed," he said. "I just wanted you to know it's war. Father's sent out the Call to Muster. The initial force—that's us—rides in five days."

Alanna's heart drummed uncomfortably. Like it or not, she would be in her first battle before she turned sixteen. "Who's commanding?" she asked.

"Uncle Gareth," was the reply. "Get your sleep. You'll need it."

∾

*A*fter several days of gathering arms and supplies and outfitting men from nearby towns and villages, the initial force was ready. Three days after the Call to Muster went out, the force assembled in military formation on the wide grass-covered hill between the palace and the Temple District, awaiting review by the King and Duke Gareth. Alanna, stationed just behind Jonathan, surveyed the ranks of men when Duke Gareth wasn't looking. *We've done pretty well for not being prepared,* she was thinking with pride, when a horse's whinny split the spring air.

Duke Gareth's chestnut, a big, good-natured animal, was pawing the air and rolling his eyes as he screamed. The puzzled Duke was fighting to get the gelding under control when his saddle slipped to the side. Gareth of Naxen fell heavily, dangerously close to his horse's thrashing hooves.

"Hold your formation!" Jonathan roared as a dozen men started forward. King Roald already had the chestnut's rein in his hand, and his servants were at the fallen man's side. Jon planted himself solidly in front of Gary, who was going to ride to his father anyway. "I *said,* hold formation!"

The big knight glared at his cousin in helpless fury; for a second Alanna was afraid he might hit

Jon. The Prince ignored the threat, adding softly, "What can you do for him that isn't already being done? We're an army, Sir Gareth; let's try and act like one!"

For a moment the tension between them held. Then Duke Gareth's son nodded grimly and returned to his place in the ranks of the knights.

Duke Baird, chief of the palace healers, was already beside Gary's father. Duke Gareth's face was white, and he was biting his lip in obvious pain. Alanna let her hands tighten on her reins until Moonlight fidgeted nervously. She could see the strange angle of Duke Gareth's left leg. When she heard shortly afterward that the Duke's leg was broken in three places and that the King would be appointing a new commander-in-chief, her feeling of doom grew. It was all too neat; so neat that she decided to miss the announcement of the new commander and pay a visit to the stables.

Handing Moonlight an apple, she whistled a brief tune. There was a noise in the hayloft, and her old friend Stefan climbed down the ladder, carrying a blanket.

"Thought ye'd be by," the hostler grunted. "Ye've a real nose fer trouble, ain't ye?"

Alanna grinned stiffly at George's man. "What makes you think I didn't come to cosset my horse?"

"Then why whistle me up?" the potbellied hostler wanted to know. "Except to chat, which ye do now an' then. Except now ye're wonderin' how

Duke Gareth's beast, what's gentler even than yer own, happened t' throw His Grace this mornin.'"

"Well, yes," Alanna admitted.

Stefan opened the folded blanket. "Mayhap I'm wrong. An' then again, mayhap this's why." He showed her a large prickly bur stuck firmly in the blanket's weave. Alanna worked it loose with difficulty. "They's a cruel scratch in th' poor beast's back where it was," Stefan went on. "An' who cinched His Grace's saddle so loose? They be so many new folk here for th' army, I don't see all as I should."

"Then none of the regular hostlers saddled Duke Gareth's horse?"

Stefan shook his head. "'Twas a newcomer. An' mayhap he was that afraid for his life when Duke Gareth was throwed, an' mayhap not. He's gone."

Alanna mulled this over, handing the blanket back to Stefan. "Thanks for keeping this for me," she said finally.

The hostler shrugged. "I knew ye'd be askin,'" he said frankly. "Best be careful, though. Us of th' Rogue knows what happens to them as asks too many questions. By the by—have ye heard who leads in Duke Gareth's place?"

Alanna shook her head.

"His Grace, th' Duke of Conté." Stefan chewed on a straw, his pale blue eyes fixed on Alanna. "Interestin', havin' a sorcerer-general, eh?"

"Very," Alanna said dryly, ignoring the sinking feeling in her stomach. She turned to go.

"Squire Alan," Stefan added, "ye might be lookin' in th' Lesser Library when ye go back. Ye've got a visitor."

Alanna hurried into the palace, the bur pricking her hand. She was surprised to find the Lesser Library occupied by a hooded monk. Getting the news from Stefan, she had expected to find someone very different.

"Excuse me," she began.

The "monk" drew back his hood and held his fingers to his lips, grinning mischievously. With an exasperated noise Alanna slammed the door and locked it behind her.

"Are you out of your mind?" she asked George in a harsh whisper. "Some of my Lord Provost's men *do* know what you look like!"

"Upset for my safety?" the thief chuckled. "I'm touched."

"You're touched in the head," Alanna snapped. "Anyway, since you're here, why *are* you here?"

"I thought you mightn't get the chance to come down to the city before you rode out, and I wanted a word with you. But *you* were wanting to ask *me* somethin'."

Alanna showed him the bur. "Stefan found this in Duke Gareth's saddle blanket. He says a new man saddled the Duke's horse, then vanished."

"And you suspect foul play," George prodded.

"Of course I do. But it doesn't make sense. Why should Tusaine go to the trouble of stopping Duke

Gareth leading the army? That won't keep us from marching the day after tomorrow."

George shook his head. "You're thinkin' like a warrior. Think like a plotter. There might be reasons closer to home as to why Duke Gareth fell from his beast."

"Closer to home?" Alanna asked.

"Who benefits?" George wanted to know. "And stop thinkin' of fightin': *start* thinkin' of power. Who gains the most power from His Grace's 'accident'?"

Alanna, about to retort that no one gained, remembered the man King Roald had appointed to Duke Gareth's place. Suddenly she swayed, feeling ill.

"Not a commander you'll be trustin' in the field, is he?" the thief asked softly.

Alanna was trembling. "I have to think about this."

George nodded. "Think on it all you may please," he said. "And watch where he places Jonathan and those loyal to Jonathan." He smoothed a hand over her coppery hair. "Would that I didn't have to stay here and keep my own in line. I mislike sendin' you there with no one to help, but there's nothin' for it. I'd be a dead Rogue if I turned my back on my folk for as long as you'll be gone. A week or two, maybe. But not a month and more."

Alanna smiled at him, wishing he *could* go with

her. Things were always clearer when George was around. "I'll be all right," she said with false assurance. "Faithful will be with me, and if things get bad I'll go to Myles. He's smart enough for three of us."

George smiled down at her, his hazel eyes still worried. "That he is. 'Twill have to do. Watch for more accidents."

"I don't think he wants to *hurt* me," Alanna demurred. "Just learn my secret."

"I believe he wants you out of the way before he goes further with his plans."

Alanna had to laugh. "What threat could I possibly be to *him?* No, I'm not as suspicious as you are, George. It must come from your line of work."

Sensing she wanted to change the subject, George shrugged. "Mayhap when Jon is king I'll be givin' up my work."

Alanna stared at him. "You're joking, surely."

The tall thief sank into a chair, watching her intently. "I'm thinkin' of turnin' respectable and takin' me a wife."

Alanna gave an ungentlemanly snort. "I like that!"

He never looked away from her. "Things look different as a man gets older."

Alanna sat on a table, swinging her feet. "I'm just having trouble seeing you turn decent citizen. Who will you give your collection of ears to? And what trade will you take up? Jewel-selling?

Returning what you stole, for a fee, of course?"

"I'm in no hurry. King Roald is a young man still. You see," he went on, "I'm waitin' for my chosen bride to grow up. She couldn't be some citizen's daughter, could she? She must be a free soul who knows my past, who doesn't care for what's proper and what's not. Someone who wouldn't scream when she opened my treasure and found the collection you mentioned."

Alanna wiped sweating palms on her tunic. She had a feeling she knew what he was leading up to, and she wished he would stop. "Good luck, George. I don't think a woman like that exists."

George stood. Gripping her shoulders, he pulled her off the table. "I've already found her, and you know it well."

Alanna glared up into his face. "You think highly of yourself!" she snapped. "I'm the daughter of a noble—"

He laughed softly. "Does that truly stand between us, Alanna? If you loved, would you care about birth or wealth?"

"Like must wed like," Alanna whispered. She wanted to run, hard and fast, and she couldn't. If he was no sorcerer, what was this spell he was weaving around her?

"There are more important things than birth. What good will a well-born husband be when you take up your shield?"

"No husband at all will do me the most good. I

don't plan to marry, and I certainly don't plan to fall in love."

"So you say now. I'm a patient man, lass. If need be, I'll wait years. And I'll not speak of this to you again. I only wanted you to know I'm yours to command." He grinned.

Alanna tried to push away. Her heart was thumping rapidly and she felt giddy. She couldn't let this go any further. "We can go on being friends like before?"

"Friends, and good ones, I trust. Confess it, lass, you'd miss me sorely, were I not about."

Alanna made the mistake of looking up into his laughing eyes. That was the problem, right there: she was not nearly ready for what she saw in his face. She looked down, afraid. "I—I won't let it ruin our friendship, George," she whispered.

"And I won't speak of it again till you ask it. Look at me, Alanna."

Alanna looked up. George kissed her, pulling her close. His mouth was warm and comforting. Alanna had not forgotten the last time, and she had discovered that she liked his kisses. Relaxing, she let her friend hold her tightly.

George pushed her away. Two spots of color burned in his cheeks. "This goes too far," he rasped. "I only—I only wanted you to know how I feel, before you go marchin' off to some battlefield."

Alanna blushed. "You pick a funny way to say goodbye, George."

He lifted a quizzical eyebrow. "Do I? Sweethearts all over the realm say goodbye in just this fashion." He kissed her once more, firmly, then went to the door, pulling up his hood.

"George?" she called softly as he released the lock. "I'll be back—and we're still friends."

He nodded and left, leaving her with far more than a loose saddle and a bur to think about.

∾

The next day Duke Roger called a meeting of his commanders. This time Alanna was present. She was relieved to learn that Gary and Raoul would be among the knights in Jonathan's personal unit, and still more relieved to know that Alex and Geoffrey would be with Roger at the fort. She and Alex were friendly once more, but she had never forgotten their "duel."

She did not feel so easy when she saw where Duke Roger planned to position Jonathan's command.

The Duke stood before a large detailed map of the Drell Valley. In the center, where the fields lining the river were the widest, blue crosses clustered along the right bank indicated the Tusaine troop camp.

"As you can see," Roger told them, pointing to the crosses, "the enemy is in place across the river from Fort Drell." Roger indicated the square on the left bank that represented the fort. "The bulk of our army will be stationed here, around and within the Fort. Lord Imrah of Legann's command will be concentrated above the fort, to the bend of the river below the Drell Falls. Below the fort Earl Hamrath of King's Reach will hold the bank down to the rapids at the end of the valley. Since the cliffs and the rapids are impassable at this time of year, we anticipate little trouble for Hamrath's men.

"At the falls themselves"—Roger's finger moved north once more, picking out the upper end of the valley—"we have an interesting situation. The river here is broad and shallow, although the current is quite strong. A determined enemy *could* cross, although there is no room on the right bank for a proper camp because of the cliffs. Raiders would have to escape the notice of every lookout above the fort; but with a foggy night and cunning, there *is* a danger. I have decided to place Prince Jonathan and his knights just below the falls. Imrah of Legann is within call if trouble arises, and for footsoldiers I am sending the present garrison of Fort Drell. They are a little battle-worn, but they are brave men. Of course we should see any enemy movement well in advance of an attempt to cross, so I feel this gives my young cousin an excellent command post without placing him in undue danger."

Alanna, standing behind Jon's chair, could feel the Prince stiffening with anger. She shot a glance at the King; Roald was nodding approval. Duke Gareth had planned to keep Jon with him at the fort so the Prince could witness first-hand how a war was waged, but Roger obviously did not feel this was necessary. The Duke of Conté went on: "Since this *is* my cousin's first command, Sir Myles will be his advisor. It is our hope, my uncle's and mine, that the Prince will listen well to a man of such wisdom."

"And very little battle experience," Alanna heard Myles mutter in his beard.

"We have but one thing to add," the King said, rising. "Until we have fully thought through the moral issues of our holding the right bank of the Drell, which was Tusaine's until our honored father's time, you have our royal command to defend the *left bank* of the river only. *You may not cross,* in pursuit or in seeking active battle."

The commanders stirred and murmured. Not cross the river? Not drive the Tusaine back to their own border? The King's voice flicked out like a lash. "We fight for the left bank only. See to it."

They all rose and bowed as the King left the room. Once the door was closed, Hamrath of King's Reach sighed. "Well, rest up, lads. It's going to be a long summer." He looked at Duke Roger. "Your Grace?"

"That is all," Roger told them. "We ride at the hour past dawn tomorrow."

∾

*T*hey rode east for twelve long days. When they finally reached the pass descending into the Drell

River Valley, Jon drew up Darkness, letting the long line of troops pass by. "Look, Alan."

Rising up below them was Fort Drell. Across the river swarmed thousands of men in Tusaine uniform, occupying their main camp. Alanna followed Jonathan's pointing finger upriver until she could see a glint of white and silver through the trees.

"The Drell River Falls," Jonathan told her. "Our new home."

Faithful, sitting in a leather cup fixed to Moonlight's saddle horn, yowled that he had preferred their *old* home. Alanna, stroking the dusty cat, had to agree. She had bad feelings about this "new home," very bad feelings indeed.

five

By the River Drell

The men who had defended Fort Drell until the arrival of the King's forces were camped below the Drell Falls, waiting for Prince Jonathan. The fact that they were veteran soldiers showed in the neatness of the camp and in the prepared look of the men. Alanna felt better when she saw them: she had a feeling these grim-faced commoners would fight well. They had spared her the work of putting up tents for Jonathan and Myles, which she appreciated. One of the soldiers, Aram, told her he was to look after the horses. All Alanna had to do was lay out Jonathan's and Myles's things, as she would be looking after both of her friends on this campaign.

When noon came, Alanna was starving. She could ride down to the fort to eat with Jon, Myles and the other knights gathered there for war councils, but she was sure she would die of hunger before she got that far. Leaving Faithful to nap on her cot, she searched the camp until she found the mess tent. The quest was easy: she followed her nose.

After filling her plate with beans and meat, Alanna sat at one of the long tables. The place on her right was soon occupied by a large foot soldier. His muscles bulged under his sturdy clothing, filling Alanna with envy, and his tanned and weathered face was framed by a thick red beard. The others greeted him eagerly, and the giant answered in a deep, rumbling voice. Alanna applied herself to her meal and listened to every word.

"What news of the enemy, Thor?" one man asked.

"No news," the giant boomed. "They're sittin' as quiet as rabbits when the hunter's by. Perhaps they'll have heard of our reinforcements."

Since only a blind man could have missed the thousand men and knights who had poured into the Tortallan camps that morning, this sally was greeted with roars of laughter.

"That'll hold them a bit," a ratty-looking man agreed when the tent had quieted. "An' you know who's in command here at the Falls? His Highness the Prince!"

The man called Thor frowned. "And this the Prince's first war command? Else they think the enemy's not plannin' much up this way—"

"Mayhap the Tusaine needed a rest from us," someone joked.

Laughing with them, Alanna choked on a bean. She coughed and swore, her eyes watering. A huge hand beating on her back nearly broke her spine.

"There, little fella. Somethin' go down the wrong pipe?" Thor asked. Alanna gasped for breath, trying to grin into the giant's bright blue eyes. Thor stared at her. "Will you look," he whispered. "The tyke has purple lamps!"

The others crowded around to see. Alanna stared back at them with wide eyes, blushing.

"And where might you be from?" Thor wanted to know.

Alanna regained her breath. "I came with the new troops this morning."

"Aren't you a mite young to be goin' to war?" the ratty-looking man asked.

Alanna stiffened proudly. "I'm sixteen next month."

"Nay!" he replied with disbelief. "You ain't more'n twelve!"

Aram pushed through the crowd and nodded to her. "No, he's near sixteen, well enough. He's the Prince's squire. I'm lookin' after their horses."

"How did a wee fella like you get to be the Prince's own squire?" Thor asked as the others muttered among themselves.

"That 'wee fella,'" someone said coldly, "is one of the best fencers at Court. He beat a full Tusaine knight in a duel last year, all by himself."

Alanna felt her hackles rising at the unknown man's tone. Thor looked up, scowling. "So you're back, Jem Tanner. Always full of the news, aren't you?"

A young man with a nasty smile sauntered over to their table. Alanna thought he might be good-looking if his eyes weren't so cold. As it was…

"Enjoying your association with us common folk, Squire?"

She didn't like him. "I *was.*"

"Leave th' lad be," someone protested.

"I just want to make sure he takes a good report back to his masters. What were you talking about? How much you liked being left to hold Fort Drell until the enemy was so entrenched that it'll take a thousand armies to dig them out? Your opinion of the King's tactics? The King's personal habits, perhaps?"

Alanna stood, her face white with anger. "I spy for no one, you remember that, *Jem Tanner,*" she snapped. "And keep a civil tongue in your head!"

The man laughed. "Big words, little fellow!"

A large hand weighed Alanna down. "Softly, lad," Thor told her. He turned to Jem. "You're right quick to pick fights with stranger-lads who're better raised than you. When will you be so quick to pick a fight with *me?*"

Jem sneered. "I was doing you a favor, warning you of the royal spy in your midst, my stupid friends." He left the tent.

Alanna drew deep breaths, fighting down her temper. The men reassured her that Jem was mean, that his words meant nothing. Only Thor was silent.

"*Are* you spyin' for His Highness?" the big man wanted to know.

Alanna grabbed her plate. "I *was* eating my lunch. I guess I'll do that somewhere else, from now on!"

Thor grinned and pulled her back into her seat. "Steady there, Squire. Can you blame us for wantin' to know? Spare me a noble's pride. Give us the news from the capital instead."

∽

*T*he routine at the falls camp was simple. Alanna looked after Jon and Myles in the morning, making sure their tents were clean and their belongings neat. She helped Aram groom the horses, taking Moonlight out for a morning ride. She ate her meals with the men; it always seemed like too much trouble to ride to the fort and join the knights. (If she realized she was avoiding Duke Roger, she mentioned it to no one.) In the afternoon she exercised, learning tricks of spear and axe fighting from Big Thor and his friends. She could hold her own among them when it came to knife fighting, and she could teach them a thing or two about the use of a sword. All things considered, she felt this was a fair exchange. Often Myles returned in the afternoon. She had history lessons from him then, something she had always enjoyed. As she got older, Myles's practical way of looking at things made more and more sense.

After the evening meal, her friends who were knights rode on patrols, and Myles and Jonathan returned to the fort to discuss tactics with Roger. Alanna remained in camp with her new friends. With Big Thor as her guide, she learned many interesting things during those long, fire-lit evenings: how to play dice without losing every copper she had; songs that would make the hardiest palace stableman turn pale; even when to keep quiet and listen. Wherever Alanna turned, day or night, Big Thor was looking after her. It was Thor who kept her from losing her temper when Jem Tanner sharpened his tongue on her, something that young man often did. Thor showed her crafty ways to handle the big weapons: the spear and the axe. On nights when the large man had riverbank guard duty, he told her stories about his days as a blacksmith in the southern hills, then as a soldier for the King.

In the two weeks after the new troops came to the valley, a number of skirmishes were fought up and down the river. There were never any direct attacks on the fort, but Hamrath and Imrah both saw daylight action. Alanna, kept at Jonathan's camp, did not fight, but the Prince did: once when he was visiting Earl Hamrath, once when he was inspecting Lord Imrah's men. Alanna always knew when there was fighting downriver, but she never could have joined her knight-master in time. Besides, good soldiers didn't leave their posts to fight somewhere else; the enemy could attack the undefended camp. Alanna could only wait and chew her nails, wondering if any of them—Jon, Raoul, Gary, or Myles—would come back.

Finally one morning she went to Duke Baird. The healers' tents lay in a broad white swath behind the fort, touched by every path that led along the river. Baird himself was taking a moment's rest when Alanna arrived. The latest fight was over, and the beds were filled with wounded and dying men.

"I'm useless upriver," Alanna told the Chief Healer flatly. "There's only Jon's or Myles's armor to clean, and I can't clean it while they're wearing it. If I don't do something, I'll scream."

The Duke looked at her. "You like to be busy, don't you, Squire Alan?"

"I don't like to waste my time. Is that the same thing?"

Duke Baird picked up a white robe and tossed it to her. "Come. I certainly won't turn you away."

Alanna followed the Duke from bed to bed, doing what he told her to do. If she had ever had a good opinion of war, it vanished by afternoon. Men died as she watched, and they didn't care about what they had fought for. They only cared about pain and the Dark God's arrival. Alanna could only help a little.

She didn't notice how much time had passed until the torches were lit. The daylight was nearly gone, and she was starting to tire. Each time she used her healing Gift, she exhausted herself a little more; but she couldn't stop, not while men were suffering.

Prince Jonathan found her bandaging a man's arm. "A fellow called Big Thor told me you were here. What are you doing?"

It took her a moment to realize someone was talking to her. "What? Oh, Jon." She wiped her forehead with the back of her hand, leaving a bloody streak. "I'm keeping busy."

"Faithful is going crazy. Myles says Faithful's afraid you'll kill yourself." Jonathan spotted Duke Baird. "Your Grace? How long has Alan been here?"

The healer glanced at Alanna. "Great Mithros, lad, I should have sent you away hours ago. You don't have the training to work so long. Prince Jonathan, get him out of here."

"Nonsense," Alanna protested, her ears roaring now that her concentration was broken. "I'm as fit as—" She stumbled, and Jon caught her.

"You certainly are," he said dryly. Ignoring her protests, he steered her out of the tent. "He's been here all day?" he asked Baird, who followed them.

The Duke nodded. "And he's saved more men than I can count. Go to bed, lad," he ordered Alanna. "You've done more than your share here. The worst is over."

Alanna was still arguing as Jon mounted Darkness and swung her up before him. "My, you're a quarrelsome little fellow," he murmured in her ear as they set off. "You're dead on your feet. Why didn't you stop?"

Alanna leaned back against her Prince, feeling very tired. Darkness, ignoring the double burden, picked his way along the river path. "They needed help," she rasped.

Jonathan nodded to Imrah's sentries as they bypassed that camp. "Why did you have to go there in the first place?"

"I wasn't useful where I was." She sighed gratefully, glad for his strong arm around her. "Hm?" she murmured.

"I *said*, must you always be useful?"

"Yes."

They rode on silently for a few moments before Jon remarked thoughtfully, "Perhaps I could make myself useful there, too, instead of attending a lot of meetings where Roger makes the decisions and never asks how I feel. Think it's worth a try?"

Alanna yawned, half-turning so her head was tucked under Jonathan's chin. "Anything's worth a try."

A yowl in the darkness greeted them as Faithful informed Alanna, *Healing is all very well, but not if you kill yourself in the process. And do you enjoy snuggling up to Jonathan like a lovesick girl?*

Alanna sat bolt upright. "Now, you listen to me, you prissy animal—" she began.

"Your Highness. You're back late." Jem Tanner, a spear in his hand, stepped out of the woods. "And

Squire Alan. Gadding about all day?"

"You've got guard duty, Jem Tanner?" Alanna snapped, aware that Jonathan was tight with anger. "Then guard."

Faithful leaped onto Alanna's lap as they rode on, startling Darkness not a bit. "Who was that?" Jonathan asked quietly.

"One of the men from camp. Being nasty is his hobby. You were warning me about him, weren't you, Faithful?"

If you're going to fall in love with the Prince, don't show it, the cat advised. *Unless you want the whole camp talking about you both.*

"I'm not fa—" Alanna stopped, aware that Jonathan was listening intently, one of his arms still around her waist.

"Are you two *talking?*" he wanted to know.

"Ask Faithful," Alanna said tersely. "I just answer his questions."

A soldier came forward to take Darkness as they entered their own camp. Myles summoned the Prince to his tent, and Alanna was left alone with her thoughts. She kept remembering the men she tried to heal, with their terrible wounds and the glazed look of pain in their eyes. She remembered every cut, every broken bone, until her stomach began to roll. She couldn't make herself think of anything else.

Her body rebelled. She rushed out to the back of the tent, where the little she had eaten that day came up violently. She struggled to be quiet; she wanted no one to witness her shame. Warriors were not supposed to throw up at the sight of blood and dying.

Cool hands soothed her head, steadying her. When she stopped heaving, Jon gave her a dipperful of water. Gratefully she splashed some on her face and rinsed her mouth out.

"If Faithful told you, I'll skin him," she whispered hoarsely.

"No," Jon replied. "I was coming back and I heard you."

"You must think I'm an awful sissy."

There was silence for a moment. Then he replied, "I threw up after my first skirmish."

Alanna looked at her friend, startled. "You never."

He nodded. "I did. I just didn't have anyone to hold my head for me." He ruffled her hair. "Don't tell the men, will you?"

"I won't tell if you won't."

"Done." He held open the flap of the tent. "It wouldn't do for them to think we're sissies, would it?"

∿

Just two nights later Alanna went looking for Big Thor. His spear needed replacing, and she had one from a man who had died in the healers' tents. The watch captain told her Thor and Jem Tanner had

guard duty on the wooded point of land just below
the camp, and Alanna set out to meet them, lugging
the too-large spear. It was late; everyone but the
sentries was going to bed. The night pressed in as
she left the camp behind. She could hear animals in
the nearby trees, even Faithful's soft padding as he
walked beside her. Suddenly the cat dashed into the
trees that screened Alanna from Thor's guard post.
Frowning, Alanna followed. She was remembering
that Jonathan had objected to this little wood that
isolated the point so effectively. The enemy could
easily cross here and pick off Jonathan's and
Imrah's men if the sentries were unable to give the
warning. Things would be easier for everyone if the
trees were chopped down. Roger had talked the
Prince out of it, saying he didn't want men tired out
with woodcutting if the enemy attacked, which
they did almost every day. His words were reasonable, and Jon had given in.

Faithful yowled a warning to Alanna before she
left the shelter of the wood. She ducked behind a
big oak and peered at the sentry post, listening.

Thor was not at his station. Neither was Jem
Tanner. Instead three men in dark clothing stood
on the point. One was lighting a torch while
another fitted an arrow to his bow. Faithful yowled
again in fury as he positioned himself between the
three and Alanna's hiding place. He hissed evilly, his
violet eyes gleaming in the darkness.

"Cursed beast!" the bowman whispered as he

let his arrow fly. It thudded into the oak's trunk, missing the cat.

"Stop it!" the third man ordered. The one with the torch was waving it over his head, signaling to the opposite bank. "Don't make so much noise!"

Alanna heard oars splashing in the river; she didn't wait to hear more. Dropping the spear, she quietly made her way free of the wood, Faithful at her heels. Once clear, she ran for all she was worth to the next guard post on the way to Jon's camp.

"Sound your horn!" she yelled to the men there as soon as she drew within earshot. She dropped beside them, panting. "Something's happened to Thor and Tanner—the enemy's crossing!"

The men sounded the alarm. Other horns in both camps took up the call as Alanna ran on to Jonathan, sending one of the sentries to alert the captains.

The Prince was dressing as she arrived. "What's up?" he asked, shrugging into his mail. Alanna told him as she handed over his weapons and his helmet. Myles came in, looking odd in plate armor.

"A messenger just got in; Imrah lost two guards as well," he said without formality. "The Tusaine is mounting a major attack between our camps. They're going to split us right down the middle; the men from the Fort may get here too late."

"We'll see," Jon said grimly. "Have the men form a half-circle around the point. We'll shove them off our ground, then help Imrah. You go on, Myles. I'm contacting Roger."

Alanna hurried outside with Myles to saddle his horse. "What's he doing?" the knight asked as she worked.

"Magic." She checked the cinches on Myles's saddle. The horse caught her tightly held excitement, fidgeting under her touch. Alanna gave Myles a hand up. "He'll send to Roger in the fire."

"Very handy," Myles approved, gripping the reins. He settled the mask of his helmet over his face and kicked his horse into a gallop. Alanna saddled Darkness, smiling grimly. It seemed even a scholar like Sir Myles became a warrior when it was necessary!

Faithful yowled at her feet as she led Jonathan's stallion around to the tent. "No," she said firmly. "You remain here. I won't have you hacked in two by someone. You can go up by the falls and watch for more trouble there; but stay away from the fighting!"

Evidently the cat realized she meant it. He trotted away, his tail high. Jonathan stepped from the tent and jumped onto Darkness's back, a shimmering silver ghost on the black horse. "I take it you told Faithful to stay out of the fighting."

Alanna double-checked the cinches of Darkness's saddle. No one would ever fall from a horse *she* had readied! "He may even obey me, for a change."

A strong hand gripped her shoulder, and she looked up into Jonathan's worried face. "I guess I can't tell you the same, can I?" he whispered.

"The biggest attack this summer, and I'm supposed to hide in my tent?" she asked, astonished. "And me your squire? Are you out of your mind?"

Trumpets were blowing, telling them the enemy was there in force, but Jonathan still hesitated. His sapphire eyes were very bright. "Against *one* warrior I can't worry about you. You've proved you can handle yourself. But against an *army*—"

She covered his hand with hers. "I have my duty, Highness. And this is *my* home, too. I'm trained to defend it, and defend it I will."

Jonathan sighed, putting on his helmet. "You know where to find me when you're armed." He urged Darkness out.

Alanna didn't waste time wondering about this strange new protectiveness in Jon. Instead she hurried to get ready. She had no armor, having refused the plate armor the weaponsmaster in the palace had offered her. (Plate was much too heavy.) Now she pulled on quilt-lined leather breeches and jacket—most foot soldiers wore the same. She was already wearing Lightning and her dagger. She stopped only to grab a shield and a short axe before hurrying outside once more. Moonlight pawed the ground, sensing action. Alanna cooed soothingly to the mare as she rapidly saddled her.

"We've got to protect Jonathan and Darkness, don't we?" She swung herself onto Moonlight's back. "Let's go, girl."

As one of the last fighters to the point, Alanna

could clearly see that the enemy had advanced past the trees, engaging Jon's men in the clearing around the main path. She glimpsed Jonathan's silver and sapphire gleaming in the thick of the battle as Darkness reared to fight as well. Myles was beside the Prince, with Gary and Raoul flanking them both. The enemy would have trouble hurting the Prince or his advisor unless they could get past two very big knights.

The patterns of the battle moved and changed before her eyes beneath the flickering torches, and Alanna clenched her teeth till her jaw hurt. The Tusaine had gotten past the Tortallans at Jonathan's back, coming around the Prince and his friends in a pincers. Shaking her head to clear it, Alanna rose in her saddle and drew Lightning.

"To me, men of Fort Drell!" she yelled furiously. "To me!"

Her friends swarmed after her, following as she charged into the thick of the fighting. The Tusaines, surprised by the unexpected attack, turned to face the slender, angry youth on the gold-and-white mare. They found themselves attacked by a troop of very tough foot soldiers and forced to give way as the youth urged his companions on.

"Alan!" someone yelled. "The knight!"

She brought her shield up instantly, just in time to intercept a hard blow from a mace. Her shield buckled a little, then held. Alanna swore as her shield arm went numb and wheeled Moonlight to face her first mounted attacker. The enemy knight was big, and he wore thick plate armor as if it was made of air. It was a struggle for her just to ward off his mace. Gripping Moonlight's reins in her teeth, she guided the well-trained mare with her knees alone, watching for an opening. As the knight lifted both arms to deliver the blow that would shatter her shield and her arm, she saw her chance. Swiftly Alanna slid Lightning into the opening between the knight's arm and chest armor, thrusting deep. With a gasp of surprise, her enemy fell from his horse, dead.

Alanna had no time now to stop and think about the first man she had killed. Jon was still in danger. She pressed forward again, the men from her camp behind her. She threw her now-useless shield into the face of an attacking knight, running him through while he was blinded. Another knight rode to engage her, swinging a two-handed sword. Alanna nudged Moonlight to the side. Gripping her axe in her left hand and Lightning in her right, she tried to circle this new attacker.

"Tortall!" The cry was loud and fierce over the crash of weapons and men's screams. "Tortall for Trebond!"

Alanna's attacker glanced at Jonathan, who was battering his way toward Alanna. Taking a chance, Alanna sent the big sword flying, wounding the knight in the shoulder in the same thrust. She pushed on to Jon's side, placing herself between

him and Myles. The men formed a circle around
them all, keeping the enemy back.

Alanna scanned the area for more trouble. In
spite of the men and knights around her prince, she
felt real danger was nearby. Something glinted in
the trees, catching her eye. An archer stood in a
maple, his arrow already on his string. His target
was Jonathan!

Alanna yelled and threw herself to one side,
knocking Jon half out of his saddle. The arrow
glanced off the Prince's shield, and one of the
Tortallan archers picked the enemy bowman out of
the tree. Alanna pulled herself upright, feeling dizzy
and tired. Her left arm—her shield arm—hurt ter-
ribly. Jonathan hauled himself back into his saddle
with Myles's help, looking at her with gratitude.
"Thanks," he said. "You—"

He was interrupted by the sound of blowing
horns. Hundreds of fresh men in Tortallan colors
poured into the clearing, led by Duke Roger. The
new troops pushed the enemy back into the woods
and onto the point, leaving Jonathan's people to
catch their wind. When the Duke of Conté
returned, his neat hair was mussed and a bloody
scratch ran down one side of his face. "They took to
their boats," he said with a grimace. "We can't follow; remember my uncle's orders."

The men began to disperse, to look after the
wounded and the dead. Alanna waited where she
was, shifting anxiously in her saddle. It was time to

look for one man in particular. Her shoulder gave a sharp, agonized pull, and she nearly fainted with pain. Its source was a deep gash down her arm; someone had wounded her without her realizing it. She needed to bandage the cut soon, but right now it was more important to attend to business. She spotted the watch captain among the healers and wounded and made her way over to him on Moonlight.

"Where's Big Thor?" she asked bluntly.

The grey-haired man looked up at her. "I'm afraid something happened to him, Squire Alan. I've been searching…" He gestured to the battle-field around them. "There's no body, nothing. Jem Tanner wandered into camp at the start of it all with a lump on his noggin. He says Thor knocked 'im out."

Alanna steadied Moonlight, who was fretting at the scent of blood from the wounded. "Jem Tanner accused Big Thor of going over to the enemy?"

The captain nodded grimly. "I don't believe him. I know Thor; he's served under me these five years. Thor don't have a treacherous bone in his body. Jem Tanner does."

Alanna frowned. "Find Jem Tanner and hold him, on my orders."

The captain bowed. "As ye say, Squire Alan."

Alanna glanced at the stand of trees, holding her wounded arm. Thor hadn't been with the enemy, or she would have heard of it by now. What if Thor had been the one betrayed, not Jem? She thought hard. If Thor was dazed or hurt, where would he go? Toward the camp—along the river-bank, perhaps?

She urged Moonlight up to the point, where still more wounded and dying men lay on the ground. Thor would be noticeable from size alone. He wasn't there. Carefully she scanned the ground until she saw what she was looking for. Something heavy had been dragged down to the river near the sentry post. Guiding Moonlight down the slope to the water's edge, she found a clump of bushes where the heavy thing had come to rest. Moonlight sniffed the dark stain on the earth there and shied away with alarm. Dismounting with difficulty, Alanna picked up some of the stained dirt and smelled it. Lately she had become too familiar with this smell: it was blood.

Dizziness made her grab Moonlight's mane, fighting to stand upright. Clenching her teeth, she found the brandy flask in one saddlebag and opened it, taking a large swallow. The harsh mouthful made her cough and sputter, but her head cleared again. She put the flask away, thinking. Thor was hurt, she knew. If this blood was his, he was badly hurt, and she couldn't waste time. Closing her eyes, she reached inside herself for the fire of her Gift. She opened her hand and let the magic flow into her palm, making it glow with a brilliant white-purple light. Opening her eyes, she nodded with grim satisfaction. The light shining from her hand was far brighter than any torch, throwing the scene around her into high relief. The effort made her head spin, but she hung on. There would be plenty of time to collapse after she found Big Thor.

Footprints were dark holes in the earth in front of her, leading north along the river to the camp, as she had suspected. With her free hand Alanna tugged on Moonlight's reins, leading the mare forward as she strained to see the prints. Once she stopped to bind up her arm. She was losing a dangerous amount of blood and the use of magic was tiring her more quickly than usual, but she was afraid that if *she* stopped looking, someone less kind might find Thor and kill him.

When Moonlight halted, Alanna nearly fell. The mare was nuzzling a huge form lying half in and half out of the river.

Alanna knelt stiffly by the body. "Thor?" she whispered. The man stirred and moaned. It was a struggle to turn him over using only one hand; her wounded arm was useless for anything but her light. Finally Moonlight helped, pushing with her nose. When they got Thor onto his back, Alanna wished they hadn't.

"Aye." The giant's voice was a whisper. "He blinded me. Have you some brandy?"

Alanna opened her flask and carefully put it to

his lips. He didn't have the strength to hold it himself.

"'Twas Jem Tanner that betrayed us," Thor rasped. "I don't know how. He was nervous from the moment we went on watch. There must've been a signal, and he hit me over the head. When I came around"—he touched a hand to his face—"I was like this, and I could hear the horns blowin'."

While Thor talked, Alanna examined him with her Gift, feeling the life slipping away from her friend. Even if his wounds had not been serious, he had lost too much blood to be healed by anyone now.

"Can you help me?" Thor whispered. "I'd just like to…go to sleep. I'm that tired."

Alanna trembled. Healing was natural for her, but she had never killed a human being with her Gift. She didn't think she could.

Thor groped until his hands found her arms. "You're hurt," he murmured, touching her already-soaked bandage. "Nay. Look after your own wounds. I'm close enough now—waitin' for the Dark God a little longer won't matter."

Alanna pressed her good hand to Thor's forehead, her Gift lighting the clearing with a deep violet fire. "Sleep, Thor," she whispered.

She felt him falling away gently, slipping into a long, dark well. Alanna rose. Thor's chest was still, and he was smiling. She smiled back at him shakily, and then the world spun; her knees trembled and gave out.

Great Merciful Mother, she thought with disgust as she fell. *I overreached myself.*

A huge shadow figure was bending over her. "Thor," she sighed, recognizing the Dark God. "You want Thor." Reaching out a hand that was blacker than night, the God touched Alanna's eyes. She closed them; if this was death, she didn't care anymore.

six

Captured!

The sun was shining when Alanna opened her eyes. Touching her dully aching arm, she found a thick bandage.

"I fixed it myself." Jonathan was sitting on a camp stool beside her. He put down his book. "I didn't think you wanted Duke Baird to get that close to you, not while you were unconscious. One of the big muscles in your arm was cut, by the way. It'll take a while to heal, even with the Gift. You're having a bad year with muscles and bones."

Alanna smiled weakly at him. "Thanks. Were you the one who found me?"

"Actually, Faithful did. You know, that cat's more intelligent than most people."

Faithful yawned. *Of course I am.* He jumped onto the foot of Alanna's bed, lying down beside her. *You've been asleep three days,* he added.

"Three days!" Alanna gasped. "That's not possible!"

"How—the cat *told* you?" Jonathan shook his head. "Never mind. I don't want to know. Yes, it's been three days. Why did you use your Gift? You were still glowing when we found you."

Alanna rubbed her head. "I had to find Thor, and there wasn't any light. And then——" Her throat was suddenly tight, and her eyes burned with tears. "I helped him sleep. The Dark God came." She looked up at Jonathan. "Have they found Jem Tanner?"

The Prince shook his head. "He's vanished. Thor was innocent?"

Taking time for sips of water, Alanna told her friend what had happened. When she finished, the Prince strode angrily around the tent.

"Treachery!" he snapped. "Merciful Mother, we should have guessed!" He sat down, suddenly dejected. "And we can't do anything about it. My father's instructions remain the same. He's even thinking of giving the right bank to Tusaine."

"If they're given the right bank, they won't stop till they have the entire valley," Alanna said frankly.

Jonathan nodded. "But no one can convince my father of that. He takes being called 'The Peacemaker' very seriously."

"He *did* establish peace after the Old King's conquests," Alanna said fairly.

"Yes, but this time he's wrong!" Jonathan growled. He brooded for a few moments before smiling and taking her hand. "Look at me. You're not awake five minutes and I'm burdening you with my problems. Mithros, I'm glad you're all right!"

Alanna squeezed his hand. "Thank you for taking care of me, Jon."

He reached over to brush a strand of hair away from her face. Suddenly he was very close. Alanna discovered she was afraid to breathe. Carefully, almost timidly, Jonathan kissed her mouth.

Someone's coming, Faithful remarked.

Myles entered the tent to find a very pale Jonathan picking up a book as his very red squire drank from a water bottle. His hazel eyes flicked from Jon to Alanna, and Alanna wondered once again how much Myles knew, or guessed, about her identity.

"It's time you came to," Myles remarked, his quiet voice even. "Do you realize you've been asleep for three days?"

∽

Using so much of her Gift when she was hurt had undermined Alanna's strength to a degree she couldn't believe possible. Duke Roger ordered her away from any fighting, leaving her to fret every time Jonathan was gone. It wasn't that she thought Raoul's squire, Douglass, couldn't look after her Prince in battle; she was just convinced he couldn't do it as well as she could. But Duke Roger had taken an interest in her welfare, and Jonathan, Myles and Duke Baird sided with him: she was in no condition to fight. Privately Alanna knew they were right: her arm would ache for months to come, and she continued to have dizzy spells. Just lighting a candle by using her Gift was more than she could manage.

Her search for something to do led her up and down the river. Finally she returned to the healers' tents; although she couldn't use her Gift, she *could* hold basins, bandage wounds and undertake countless little tasks during those long June days after her sixteenth birthday. Jonathan often came for her there and stayed, talking to the men and doing some healing of his own.

Sometimes the healers shooed her away, particularly if Duke Baird noticed she was tiring. She tried the weapons-smiths then. These gruff men would ignore her except to shove a pair of bellows or an extra set of tongs into her good hand, motioning for her to make herself useful. She mended swords, spears, knives and armor, learning how to put a keen edge on a blade and how to keep a fire at the same heat for an hour or more. She would never be as adept as Coram, who had taught her the basics of the blacksmith's art, but she would always be able to keep her equipment in good working order.

She also signed on as a sentry. Jonathan's men had suffered the worst losses in the big Tusaine attack, and they welcomed even one small relief guard.

One evening in late July she and Faithful were standing watch just below the falls. They were alone at the moment. The soldier sharing the watch with them was having trouble with a healing leg, and Alanna had sent him back to camp for a replacement. He had not been gone long when a twig snapped behind them. Alanna spun, leveling her spear at her visitor.

Orange light flared against a hand, making Duke Roger's face briefly visible. Faithful pressed against Alanna's ankles, hissing and spitting.

"Stop it," Alanna told him, slowly lowering the spear. Faithful obeyed. "Your Grace. Aren't you out late?"

"Not really. Sit down, please. I know you still tire easily."

Alanna obeyed, sitting on a large rock. Faithful hopped up onto her lap. "I'm honored by Your Grace's concern."

"You did a brave thing, tracking down the man Thor and hearing his story. It's a pity you collapsed before you made it back to camp; you might have captured the traitor."

Alanna shrugged without taking her eyes off Jonathan's cousin. "Don't think I haven't kicked myself about that, sir, several times."

Silence fell between them, stretching out over endless moments. *I won't ask why he's here,* Alanna told herself grimly. *He'll get to it in his own time. He didn't come up here just to be polite.*

Suddenly Duke Roger said, "We are not friends, are we, Alan?"

Alanna tightened her hands on her spear. This

was coming to grips with a vengeance! "No, Your Grace, we're not," she replied evenly.

Without the light of his Gift it was hard to read the Duke's face. "Might it be possible we are enemies?"

Alanna thought about his, and about his reasons for asking. "I don't know," she said finally. "Perhaps *you* should tell *me*."

"I could be a very good friend, Alan."

Her throat was dry. What kind of game was he playing? Was this a warning—or a threat? "I have no desire to make you my enemy, sir. I'd like to live to a ripe old age and die in my sleep."

White teeth flashed in a grin against his shadowed face. "I can sympathize. Such an ending could be yours—if we were friends. *Many* things could be yours."

Alanna shifted her hold on the spear; her fingers were getting numb. "I would have to be assured that my other friends have the same chance, Your Grace," she said boldly. "Frankly, I doubt that's your aim."

For a long moment he said nothing. Then she saw his broad shoulders lift in a shrug. "I see. Thus, as long as you feel this way, we will be…"

"Less than friends," Alanna supplied diplomatically.

Roger bowed. "I appreciate your honesty, Alan of Trebond. Not many dare be so open with me."

She smiled crookedly. "Not many have insanity in their families, either."

This drew a laugh from him. "I see. Well—good night to you, Squire Alan."

Alanna stood, a little stiff from the dampness of the river. "Your Grace." She watched Roger fade into the shadows. "He has style," she remarked quietly.

Style or not, he's as treacherous as a snake, Faithful warned her.

Alanna touched the ember-stone under her shirt. "I know," she replied softly. "I just wish I had something to crush him with."

Give him time, the cat meowed. *He'll give you plenty to crush him with.*

Alanna frowned. "The problem is that by the time he does he'll probably be invincible."

True. Faithful yawned. *Fog's rising.* And with that he curled up and went to sleep.

Alanna watched the ghostly white tendrils rising from the river's surface, feeling very tired. "Just what I need," she yawned disgustedly. "I didn't think there'd be any fog tonight."

The mist rose quickly, smothering all the night noises. Everything sounded different: the river, the distant camp, even the nearby waterfall. Alanna's nose itched till her eyes watered. She felt like lying down right there and taking a nap. That would never do: she was on sentry duty! Where was the other guard? One should have come by now. Nervous, Alanna made her way to the river and splashed her face with cold water. That helped a little. Returning to her post, she discovered that she couldn't waken Faithful. Something was very wrong; the itching of her nose meant sorcery, and Faithful seemed to be its victim. Should she go for help?

The rock striking her head settled the question. Alanna dropped, and the men who had crept up behind her in the fog chuckled grimly.

"Hurry!" Jem Tanner hissed as they tied her hands and feet. "We won't be safe from the spell much longer!"

"What about the cat?" one of the men yawned. "He said to—"

"Forget the cat!" Jem snapped. "Just get the boy into the boat with the others!"

∾

A sentry on the second watch ran into camp, Faithful limp in his hands. "Squire Alan's been kidnapped!" he told the Prince, gasping. "The cat—he's alive, but I can't wake him! And the other guard who went out with the squire—he's lyin' in his tent. I can't wake him either!"

Jonathan took Faithful, reaching with his Gift into the sleeping animal. Without warning, his eyes rolled up and he collapsed. Faithful stirred and went back to sleep.

The sentry brought Myles on the run. The knight wasted no time: he seized the water bucket and threw the contents over both Jon and Faithful. The cat only turned over and sighed. The Prince stirred, gazing sleepily up at his friend. "Sorcery," he whispered, sitting up. "Sorcery meant to make the cat sleep…" He grabbed the sentry, his face white. "Alan was *kidnapped?* You're sure?"

The watch captain ran into the tent. "Your Highness, Sir Myles—we're missing three men along the river—two foot soldiers, Micah and Keel, and—"

"Alan of Trebond," Myles said grimly.

"Aye, sire. This blasted fog's so thick you can barely see your hand before your face, but we found tracks. The sneaks landed below Micah's post and worked their way to the falls, taking those three. I've got men watching for an attack now, and the camp's on alert."

Faithful struggled to his feet and shook himself, his fur sticking out in wet points. Suddenly he let out a yowl of fury and dashed into the night. Myles and the soldiers stared after him in amazement.

"Someone knew he'd be on watch with Alan," Jonathan said. Suddenly he looked old and grim. "They laid a magic that would affect Faithful in particular. When I touched him, I went under." He bit his lip. "They may've taken three, but they *wanted* Alan. They knew he'd be there with his cat, and they took him." He gripped Myles's arm. "Myles, we have to *do* something! If they find out—"

"Hush, Jonathan!" Myles interrupted. "We'll do all we can."

The sentry who brought Faithful cried out,

"And that's *nothing!* We're bound here by the stupidest lot of orders ever writ—" His captain and two noblemen were staring at him. He gulped and continued, "Saving your presence, Highness, my lord, but it's true. Micah and Keel are chums of mine, and Squire Alan saved this eye, not two weeks ago, and we can't help them!"

Jonathan put a hand on the man's shoulder, smiling tightly. "We'll see, my friend." He nodded to Myles. "I'm off to the fort. Maybe Roger will have some idea of what's going on."

Myles tugged his beard. "That's possible," he said thoughtfully. "That's very possible."

～

*R*oger knew nothing other than the kind of spell that had been used on the cat and the sleeping guard. "Any village healer can do it, I'm afraid," he told Jonathan grimly. "Sleep is particularly easy to create, because it is something the body does naturally." He gazed out the window and sighed, knowing Jonathan was watching him closely. "A pity about that young man. With your father's orders… We'll have to wait for a ransom demand. Alan's obviously a noble, and even Duke Hilam won't dare to flout the conventions of war."

But no ransom demand came by messenger bird across the river. It was well past noon on the day after the kidnapping when a red-eyed Jonathan returned to his tent. Faithful lay on the cot beside him, looking lost. Jon fell asleep while petting the cat, but within a few hours he was prowling the riverbank like a restless tiger. Other men were there—men from the camp, weapons-smiths, healers, Jonathan's friends—all staring at the other side, as if they could see the missing three if they looked hard enough. When Jonathan returned to camp, he found Myles staring into a full mug of brandy. To his surprise, the shaggy knight wasn't drinking.

"This is too serious for drink," Myles said, guessing the Prince's thoughts. He nodded toward Faithful; the cat was lying with his head on his paws, his eyes wide and unblinking. "He's worried. That makes *me* worried. I can't be convinced that Alan's capture was not the sole object of this raid."

Jonathan sat down, twisting his hands together. "Myles, I *can't* leave him over there," he whispered. "He—"

Myles shook his head. "Don't."

"Sir?"

"You're about to tell me why Alan of all people should not be left among enemies for very long. I would rather hear it from Alan, when he's ready to tell me."

"You already know," Jonathan accused.

The older man smiled. "Let's say I've formed an educated guess. I can wait to have it confirmed."

Jonathan scowled, rising to pace again. "If Alan stays on that side of the river, you won't have to wait much longer."

Myles saw Jon was eyeing the river. "Your father was very specific, Prince Jonathan," he pointed out softly. "It would mean the head of any man who tried to rescue them. I hope you'll warn the others, because I'm afraid a rescue is exactly what they have in mind."

Jonathan stared at Myles. Suddenly he had an idea, a wild idea, but an idea nonetheless. "Perhaps the punishment would depend on who led the rescue!"

Myles met his stare with calm eyes. "I would be obligated by my oath to your father to stop a rescue attempt."

Jonathan smiled, knowing what the knight was really saying. "Of course, Myles. Oh, what will you be doing after the evening meal?"

Myles tugged his beard. "I think I'll ride down to the fort to confer with our commander. I shall probably be there very late."

Jonathan nodded absently. "You should take a couple of men," he murmured, thinking hard. "We don't want *you* kidnapped, with our security so poor." He strode off, his walk purposeful.

Watching him go, Myles began to chuckle. "That young man gets more like the Old King every day."

The cat stretched, suddenly looking better. *Yes,* he agreed.

〜

Jonathan discussed his plan with only one of the men: the soldier who had brought Faithful the night before. He was enough. When Jon, Gary,

Raoul and their squires arrived at the falls just after sunset, they found thirty grim-faced men—and Faithful—waiting.

"So many?" Sacherell whispered nervously.

"That's the smallest number I could manage," the young soldier replied. "I've got ten more standing guard against our return."

Jonathan nodded, pleased. "Let's move."

Myles and Roger were playing chess when a guardsman burst in to whisper hurriedly into Roger's ear. Myles saw with interest that Jon's cousin suddenly turned white.

"*What?*" the Duke snapped.

The guardsman bowed. "It's true, Your Grace. More than thirty of them, I'd guess. They've fired the huts the enemy built on the north side of their camp. I saw it myself from the wall."

Jumping to his feet, Roger turned on Myles, his eyes burning. "Do you know what my precious cousin has done? He's trying to rescue that bedamned squire of his!"

Myles sipped his wine. "Has he indeed?" the knight replied mildly. "The King will not be pleased."

"How could you not hear of this?" Roger demanded hotly. "You were there all afternoon. Surely you must have seen them plotting!"

"They wouldn't tell their plans to anyone who would stop them," Myles said. "I knew they were upset, of course. It *is* natural for men to be angry when three comrades are snatched from under their very noses. There are even rumors that Jem Tanner was not the only traitor among us."

"Shall I assemble a helping force, Your Grace?" the guardsman wanted to know. "They must be outnumbered—"

"Don't be a fool!" Roger snapped. "It'll be *our* heads with the King if we further my cousin's folly."

"I doubt His Majesty will have Jonathan beheaded for rescuing a friend," Myles commented. "I also doubt that he will be so unfair as to punish the Prince's companions." He disappeared into his wine cup.

Roger drew a deep breath before answering, finally retrieving his iron self-control. "What my cousin may do, others may *not* do." He turned to the guardsman. "Post archers along the riverbank. They can cover Prince Jonathan's retreat." He stalked over to his desk to grab his seeing-crystal. "I must inform my uncle. If you will excuse me, Sir Myles?"

∾

Alanna came to in a small wooden hut. Two other men, Micah and Keel, were there, but they were still unconscious. Glancing at the tiny, iron-barred window, she saw it was well past noon. She drew a dipper of water from the bucket, splashing it in the men's faces with difficulty. This was due in part to the stiffness in her wounded arm and in part to the fact that she, like the two men, was wearing heavy chains. Calling on the small reserve of magic she had built up over the weeks of rest to stop the pounding in her head and arm, she found herself weak and gasping. There was magic in her chains, magic that bound her Gift as well as the rest of her.

Micah and Keel came around slowly, still dazed from the sleeping-spell.

"Sorcery—fah!" Keel growled, spitting on the ground. "No decent warrior uses sorcery!"

"No decent warrior uses traitors, either," Micah told his comrade. "And Duke Hilam's done both. He'll stop at nothing."

They were interrupted by heavy footsteps and the clank of a key ring. The door swung open, revealing a Tusaine captain flanked by two soldiers. He pointed to Micah and Keel.

"You two. You'll be paid well and released, if you give information."

Micah jerked his head at Alanna. "What about the boy? He's a noble; he's got the right to be ransomed."

The captain shook his head. "Not that one. His Grace wants to talk with him personal." He scowled. "A filthy way to fight a war," he muttered.

Alanna and her two friends exchanged puzzled looks. What was the man talking about?

"You will have your lives if you tell us what we want to know," the Tusaine went on.

"I'd sell my own mother's honor first," Keel

snapped. "What are you going to do with Squire Alan?"

The captain shrugged. "You had your chance." He nodded to his men, and the three left, locking the door behind them.

"That was very well said," Alanna remarked slowly, "but I have a feeling you just gave away your lives."

"Mayhap our people will try a rescue," Keel said hopefully.

Alanna shook her head. "The King gave orders. Anyone who tries a rescue will be guilty of treason."

"Give me a hand up," Micah ordered Keel suddenly. "I want to see something."

Alanna watched as the younger man boosted Micah up to the window. Finally Micah jumped down. "If we could get loose, we're to the rear of the camp," he said gruffly. "There's nothing between us and the trees. We're hid away from their main army, Squire Alan." He shook the chains on his arms. "If we weren't burdened with these…"

"Oh!" Alanna hit herself on the forehead. "I'm stupid as well as insane. Here." She pulled a long strip of metal from its hiding place inside her belt and went to work on the locks. "The second you have a chance, break for the trees and make your way back. That's an order, understand?"

"But…" Micah protested as his chains fell to the ground.

"Don't say 'but.' It's me they want. If you get

free, they may not chase you very hard. Prince
Jonathan has to know what happened." She began
on Keel's chains as Micah rubbed his ankles, frowning.

"Where did you learn this?" Keel asked.

Alanna laughed shortly. "You'd be surprised."
Once Keel's chains were undone, she tried the lockpick on her own. She half-expected the result: the
pick turned white-hot. Alanna dropped it on the
ground where it lay, melted out of any useful shape.

"As I thought. Somebody made triply sure I
couldn't leave." Was it just an accident that her
chains alone were sorcerer- and pick-proof? Somehow she had trouble believing it was coincidence.

More visitors came as sunset was dying from
the sky. At the sound of approaching footsteps,
Micah and Keel hid themselves on either side of the
door, their chains ready for use as weapons. The
footsteps stopped.

"Captain," a male voice hissed, "if you continue
your objections, I will see to it that you're given a
less unpleasant command—under the noses of the
fort archers, for example."

"I don't like fighting a war this way." It was the
voice of the captain who had first visited them. "It
isn't honorable."

"I believe in *results*, not honor." The stranger
uttered three arcane words. Red fire burst through
the hut, blinding Alanna. Micah and Keel slumped
to the floor, unconscious, and the door swung

open. Alanna blinked the spots from her eyes as a richly dressed nobleman, accompanied by the captain and two large soldiers, walked in. The nobleman was not much taller than Alanna, with large hazel eyes and a sharply handsome face. His looks were spoiled by the ugly set of his mouth as he prodded Keel with an elegantly shod toe.

"I thought something like this might occur. Who picked the locks?" His beautiful eyes flicked at Alanna. "You?"

Alanna stood braced, her arms folded across her chest. "Who wants to know?"

The nobleman smiled cruelly. "I've heard about your bad manners, Alan of Trebond."

"Funny. *I* always heard the men of Tusaine possessed some trace of honor." She glanced at the captain, who was turning beet red. "Isn't it odd how rumor lies?"

Someone else stepped through the open door. "Don't let him get the upper hand, brother," Jem Tanner warned. "He's tricky."

Alanna leaped for Big Thor's murderer. The guards caught her and slung her to the ground, where one of them pressed his spear to her throat. "Don't do it again," he advised gruffly. After a moment he raised the spear, letting Alanna sit up. Jem retreated to the door, white under his tan.

"Kill the little viper, Hilam!" he urged. Micah and Keel were coming to. "Before he finds a way to trick you!"

Alanna looked at the well-dressed man. So *he* was Duke Hilam, the one responsible for this long, hateful summer. It was hard to believe so much trouble could come from such a small man.

Duke Hilam covered a yawn. "I'll kill him when I'm ready, brother," he announced. "Not a moment sooner."

Alanna stared. "You're *brothers?*"

"There isn't much of a family resemblance." Hilam grinned cruelly. "That's what made Jemis an ideal spy."

Then Alanna remembered that the three royal brothers of Tusaine were King Ain, Duke Hilam, and Count Jemis. Jemis—or Jem—was rarely seen in public because he rode around the land, sending reports to Prime Minister Hilam. A spy indeed!

Boiling mad, Alanna struggled to her knees. "Forgive me for not recognizing you sooner, Duke Hilam," she spat. "Your sweet nature should have—"

Hilam kicked her down. "I'm not amused by you, *prisoner*. Don't try my patience."

Alanna curled up around the side he had kicked, sweating with pain. No one was watching her two companions; all attention was on her and the Duke. She looked up at him, boiling mad. "You *are* brave, kicking a chained prisoner. They must sing heroic ballads about you on winter nights!"

Hilam grabbed her chains, yanking her to her feet. "I've heard about your tongue, Squire." He was smiling calmly; *that* frightened her. No one as angry as Hilam smiled, unless he was insane. "Perhaps I'll cut it out." He threw her against the rear wall and advanced on her.

Alanna struggled to her feet, never taking her eyes off him. "Behavior I'd expect from the goatherd's bastard, not a nobleman," she taunted as Micah and Keel inched toward the open door. "Perhaps your mother tricked your father?"

Hilam hit her again, knocking her to her knees. Micah and Keel bolted out the door, running for all they were worth. When Hilam turned to follow, Alanna grabbed him, wrapping her arms around his torso. The Tusaine was stopped from throwing a spell after the escaping men by the magic that kept Alanna helpless.

"Don't follow!" Hilam ordered, yanking out of Alanna's hold and slapping her. "*This* is the one we have to worry about!"

"Let me have him," Jemis urged. "He's been an annoyance to me for a long time. I could have killed Prince Jonathan that night if he hadn't been there."

Alanna could hear shouting in the distance. She crossed her fingers and prayed her friends would escape.

"He's been an annoyance to many for a long time," Hilam snapped, his clean-shaven face grim. "Before I let you play with him, he's going to tell me something about Tortall. He's going to tell me all Prince Jonathan's plans and all King Roald's plans.

Then he will tell me things that don't interest me at all, but he'll tell them because he'll say anything to stop the pain."

"Pigs might fly," Alanna snapped. She spat in the man's face.

Hilam wiped the spit away, his lovely eyes thoughtful. "You'll take a while to break." He smiled suddenly, and her stomach sank. "That will be quite enjoyable. Only think, you'll have the doubtful fame of being the one responsible for my taking this entire valley. How does *that* sit with your much-loved honor, Squire Alan?"

"Perhaps your mother betrayed your father with a warthog," Alanna said thoughtfully. She would just get sick if she listened to what he was saying. "You both certainly have a warthog's manners. Jem there even has a warthog's looks."

Jem lunged for her, only to be stopped by one of the guardsmen.

"Jemis is very rash," Hilam told Alanna. "I'm not. It's going to take far more than these little barbs to pierce *my* armor—"

"Perhaps my sword will pierce it, then?" Jonathan asked coolly from the doorway. "Thank you, Faithful. You seem to have led us to the right place."

Micah, Keel, Gary, Sacherell, Raoul and Douglass were behind the Prince. Faithful ran between their feet to place himself between Alanna and her tormentor, hissing angrily. Hilam, unnerved by the cat's purple stare—so like Alanna's own—stepped back into Sacherell's grip.

Jonathan laid the point of his sword beside Hilam's nose. "Don't move, please, and don't try any sorcery. I'll make you swallow it." He turned to the three soldiers, who were watching Gary's and Raoul's drawn bows with keen attention. "The keys to my friend's chains. Now."

The captain tossed them to Alanna, who grinned at him before setting to work on the locks. "Jonathan, the soldiers are all right. But these two"—she pointed to Hilam and Jemis—"are King Ain's brothers."

"Jem Tanner, a king's brother?" Micah gasped.

A slow grin spread across Jon's face. "I think I know how we are going to leave this camp safely. We're taking two guests with us, two very *important* guests. And I'm sure we can think of a fair ransom. Don't you, Duke Hilam? I know King Ain will not think peace is not *too* small a price to pay, not for his brothers' lives."

King Roald was not pleased, but—as Myles and Jonathan had known—he could scarcely behead his own son. Instead Roald negotiated the Drell Peace, in which Tusaine vowed to relinquish all claims to the valley forever. King Ain was willing to agree to much more: he wanted his brothers back to rule his lands for him. By the end of August the peace was signed, and Alanna and her friends were able to go home.

seven

Winter Lessons

*A*lanna pulled her cloak tight against the wind and knocked hard on the door marked with the healer's sign. She waited, watching the last fall leaves dance in the street, until Mistress Cooper appeared.

"Hello," Alanna said shyly, letting the hood fall back from her face so George's mother could see who her late-night visitor was. "Can we talk?"

Mistress Cooper smiled, motioning Alanna inside. "It's been a long time, little one," she commented as she bolted the door. "Come into the kitchen and I'll make us some tea." She led the way, her majestic form casting a long shadow in the hallway. "I trust you're recovered from your wounds? How is your arm?"

Alanna took off her cloak and draped it in front of the kitchen fire before rotating her left arm obediently. "It's a little stiff sometimes, but it's all right now. I wasn't as badly hurt as people think."

Mistress Cooper put on the teakettle. "My son doesn't feel as you do. But perhaps he has his reasons for worrying?"

The girl blushed. "George worries about me too much. I hope he gets over it before I go away."

"So you still plan to leave us once you have your shield?" The woman moved around the room on silent feet, getting cups and a plate full of cakes. Alanna bit into one of the cakes eagerly; she had only picked at her dinner.

"Of course," she said, her mouth full. She swallowed quickly. "I have a feeling that when I tell them I'm a girl, they won't want me around."

"Could be you're not doing them justice," Mistress Cooper suggested, pouring out the tea. "George tells me you're liked and trusted."

Alanna frowned. "Not by all." Shoving Duke Roger to the back of her mind, she cradled the cup of tea in her hands.

"How is His Highness?" the woman asked, sitting down.

Stirring the tea with the tip of her finger, Alanna replied softly, "I'm not sure. He's been— very odd lately. Ever since we returned from the Drell Valley."

"How so?"

"He—he blows hot, then cold. Sometimes I'm his best friend in the world. And sometimes he acts as if I'm poison. It doesn't make sense. He—" Alanna blushed. "He kissed me, this summer. I think he *wants* to do it again, except he doesn't. Sometimes he talks as if he doesn't like George, except I know that isn't true, because he comes into the city to see George when I'm occupied. He expects a lot from a person!" Alanna burst out, getting up to pace. "If I go to social events with him—and he *makes* me go—I have to have every hair in place. I have to have better manners than everyone else. I have to dance with all the ladies, as he does, even though no one else has to. I tell him I feel like a fool, and he tells me it's better to be a fool who's considerate than a fool who isn't. But if I really talk to a lady—or even to Gary or Raoul—for a bit, he gets angry! He says I mustn't lead the ladies on, and he accuses me of flirting with Gary and Raoul in the same breath!" Alanna sat down and gulped her tea, surprised at how the words had tumbled out of her.

"You seem rather angered with Prince Jonathan," Mistress Cooper observed.

Alanna turned deep red. "I don't know how I feel," she muttered. "I just can't figure out why he's treating me this way. But that isn't what I came about." She drew a deep breath. "Would you teach me how to dress like a girl?"

Mistress Cooper raised her eyebrows. "Now, this is odd," she said calmly. "Why such a request?"

Alanna made a face. "I don't know. I just—I see all the Queen's ladies wearing pretty things, and I've been thinking lately I like pretty things. I'm going to have to be a girl someday. Why shouldn't I start practicing now?"

If Mistress Cooper thought Alanna's sudden wish to look pretty had anything to do with

Jonathan, or with George, she knew better than to say so. Instead she agreed to help Alanna with her new project, beginning that very night by taking the girl's measurements.

ᴄᴡ

Several days later, Alanna came to Mistress Cooper's for fittings. As the older woman adjusted a hem, Alanna twisted, trying to see her back in the long mirror. "Hold still," Mistress Cooper ordered, her mouth full of pins. "You're worse than a city lad getting fitted with his first pair of long breeches."

"It doesn't look right," Alanna objected, trying to hold her body rigid while she turned her head. "It looks like Squire Alan in a girl's dress."

"That's because we've done nothing with Squire Alan's hair. Hold still!"

The dress properly fitted, Mistress Cooper fussed with the girl's flaming locks and put some cosmetics on her flinching face. "I think you're wise to start accustoming yourself to woman's gear," she commented as she brushed dark color over Alanna's eyelids. "Although you've a lot to learn."

"If I'd known it was going to be this much fuss, I never would've asked," Alanna muttered. Her friend laughed. "It's just…I needed an adventure. I've been pretty restless lately."

"Life in the palace is too tame for you?" Mistress Cooper asked sympathetically.

"Not too *tame,* precisely," Alanna objected. "I

just need to *go* somewhere. I need to get away from—certain people." She didn't want to say that Jonathan had kissed her again only the night before. She didn't even want to remember it, because when she did she also remembered the strange and frightening excitement she had felt when he held her. Now she sighed, confused.

"I need time to think about things."

"I see," Mistress Cooper replied. "Well, stand up, child. Let me look at you."

Alanna stood, patting her pinned-up hair and tugging her skirt. Mistress Cooper had a very odd look on her face.

"Is something wrong?" Alanna asked nervously.

The older woman made her face the mirror. Alanna swallowed. She was looking at a *lady*.

"I'm beautiful," she whispered in awe.

Mistress Cooper laughed at this. "You'll pass," she said, pushing Alanna into the kitchen. "You're not as beautiful as Lady Delia, say, or the new lady at Court, Cythera of Elden."

Alanna sighed. "*Nobody's* as beautiful as the Lady Cythera," she said dryly. She moved to sit down.

"Not that way!" Mistress Cooper cried in alarm. "You'll rumple your skirts! Sweep them out—like this—and sit with them spread around you. And keep your feet together."

Alanna tried this. It took several attempts before she got it right. "It's going to be as hard to learn to be a girl as it was to learn to be a boy."

"Harder," the woman said, putting the tea on. "Most girls don't have to unlearn being a boy. And now you have *two* sets of Court manners to master."

"But I already *know* Court manners," Alanna protested, getting the cups down.

"Do you know the different kinds of curtsy?" Alanna shook her head. "How to write invitations?" Alanna shook her head. "How do you accept an offering of flowers from a young knight, or a married man?"

"As if I'd be getting flowers from anybody!" Alanna snorted. She rummaged in the cupboards. "Any cakes left?"

"I baked some fresh—"

"Great Merciful Mother!" Alanna gasped. She could hear horses in the courtyard: visitors! Her hand flew to the ember-stone and her pregnancy charm, both now revealed by the low neckline of her dress. Turning, she ran for the door leading to the rest of the house.

Mistress Cooper caught her. "What has gotten into you?"

The kitchen door opened. "Mother, see who I finally brought to meet you!" George called. He turned to someone still outside. "Come on in, then—she's here."

"Stand straight," Mistress Cooper told Alanna. "Face him. You'll have to do it sometime."

Alanna drew a breath and turned around. George was still looking outside. "The man will take care of your horse; that's what he's there for," he told his companion. He looked back at his mother. "I'm sorry. I didn't know you had—"

The King of the Thieves stopped talking abruptly. His eyes widened. Carefully he looked Alanna over, inch by inch, while the girl turned a deep red. "It's not polite to stare," she said tartly.

"George, you're blocking the way." Someone behind the thief laughed. Alanna turned pale. She knew that voice. "Have you changed your mind? You don't want me to meet your mother after all?" Prince Jonathan, dressed in the plain shirt and breeches he always wore into the city, edged into the kitchen behind the thief.

Mistress Cooper moved forward, smiling. "And so you're Prince Jonathan, or is it Johnny today?"

"I'm always Johnny in the city," Jonathan admitted.

Alanna put her hands on her hips, scowling. "And do you mention the fact in front of every strange young lady you meet?" she demanded.

Jonathan looked at her, a small frown crossing his face. "Forgive me, gentle lady. I didn't see…" His voice trailed away as he stared. Finally he whispered, "You—you're wearing a dress. You look—" He blushed, swallowed and changed the subject. "Where did you get the stone around your neck? I haven't seen it before."

"Close the door," Mistress Cooper ordered him. "You're letting the cold in. Lass, we'll need two more cups, I think."

George gripped Alanna's arm as she moved past him. "So you're a girl, after all."

"I thought you knew that," Alanna snapped. She looked at Jonathan. "*You* don't seem surprised."

He grinned. "Oh, I am, a little, I knew you were up to something, though. You've been awfully mysterious lately. And remember I caught you two days ago piling your hair on top of your head looking at yourself in the mirror."

"Some people think they're pretty observant since they became heroes of the war," Alanna said, sniffing.

"Maybe I do," Jonathan replied amiably. "But what is that stone?"

Alanna looked at the ember-stone, fingering it "I got it from—from a lady I met once."

Jonathan frowned. "Why would a lady give you a charm? It looks valuable, whatever it is; and it's magic for certain."

Alanna shrugged. "If it's magic, it's not magic I can use. And she gave it to me—well, it's a long story, and I really don't want to tell it right now. I don't understand it myself." She sat down, and Mistress Cooper handed her the teapot.

"Pour," the woman instructed. "You two can take off your hats, at least. Don't you know when you're being served by a lady?"

ᵔᵔ

*I*t was not the last time Alanna wore a dress. Wearing a black wig, she went into the city (usually in Mistress Cooper's company), getting used to her skirts and learning about the things most girls her age took for granted. They had the most fun in the marketplace, where they often shopped for additions to the wardrobe Alanna kept in a locked chest at the foot of her bed.

Snow came in mid-November, falling for days and forming immense drifts. The people watched and prayed for a break in the weather. It finally came, and the snow ceased to fall, leaving in its place bitter cold that refused to break. Huntsmen called it "Wolf Winter," the time when wolves, finding little else to hunt, turned on men. Alanna, loathing the cold, bundled up and tried her best to ignore it.

In early December the first reports of wolves came from the villages around the Royal Forest. The King sent hunt after hunt to slay the man killers, while other fiefs in the north of Tortall reported the same problem. Coram wrote that he had moved the families of Fief Trebond in to the castle to keep them safe. There was certainly room enough, he added in his letter, but it was annoying to have so many children underfoot.

By February most of the killers were slain or in hiding, except one. He was called Demon Grey. He

had been wounded at least three times—a huntsman's arrow had even taken one of his eyes
recently—but nothing seemed to stop him for long,
for he continued to prey on the villages of the Royal
Forest. When at last he entered a woodsman's hut,
taking away a baby girl, the King ordered every
man in the palace who could carry a spear out for
the hunt. Duke Roger came, splendid in ermine-
trimmed green velvet. Duke Gareth was there, his
bad leg still a little stiff. Even Myles was present,
warm in brown velvet and fur and looking uncomfortable. The King himself led the hunt.

Alanna was even more uncomfortable than
Myles. Moonlight had cast a shoe; Alanna couldn't
ride her. Instead she was mounted on a prickly
chestnut with a hard mouth, a fidgety, anxious fellow who obviously preferred his nice warm stall.
Alanna didn't blame him. She dressed to survive
the weather, with several layers of wool clothing
and fleece-lined leather over it all. When she
checked herself in the mirror, she was several sizes
larger.

"We're going to hunt, not sleep out all night,"
Jonathan said, laughing when he saw her.

Alanna blushed. "I get cold."

"I don't think you can move with all those layers on," he told her as they waited in the courtyard
for his father to arrive.

"Oh?" Leaning from the saddle in a swift movement, Alanna scooped up a handful of snow and

lobbed it into her Prince's face. "See?" She grinned as she trotted past Jonathan. "I'm warm *and* mobile."

She caught up with Gary and Raoul, riding with them for a while. She saw little of her large friends these days; the King always had duties for them. The three laughed and joked until the Huntsman-in-Charge blew the Discovery up ahead. Then the knights rode on while Alanna stayed back, knowing she wouldn't be needed. She didn't mind if someone else got the glory in a hunt of this size. Too often she felt sorry for the animal, outnumbered by so many armed and trained knights (not that she could feel sorry for a child-killing wolf).

The discovery *was* a wolf. The King brought it down himself. But it was not Demon Grey. Alanna watched every movement between the trees, wishing she had brought Faithful. It had seemed silly in the morning to bring a cat on a wolf hunt, but now she missed her companion's sharp ears and nose.

The hunt moved on, bagging another wolf and a mean old boar. Slowly the hunters spread over the Royal Forest, until occasionally Alanna followed it by sound alone. When it swept around her, she would fall in with the others, then the hunters would ride on. She wasn't worried. She was never so far away that a blast on the horn hanging at her waist wouldn't bring someone immediately, and there were usually other horsemen around. Besides, Demon Grey attacked children and old people, not warriors.

A sound—crashing! A wolf's snarl! Wheeling the chestnut, Alanna yelled for help. After an answering triumphant shout, she spurred into the clearing where the shout seemed to come from and halted. Duke Roger knelt in the snow, his spear fixed in the body of a giant grey wolf. He grinned when he saw Alanna. "A few moments earlier, and *you* might have had him, Alan."

Alanna dismounted, ready to give the Duke a hand. "I don't grudge you the kill, sir. Are you certain that's Demon Grey?"

Roger shrugged. "How many wolves of this size and description can there be?" he asked.

A low snarl struck Alanna's ears. Her horse reared and bolted with a whinny of terror, taking her spear with him. Alanna froze, swearing under her breath and peering closely at the surrounding trees. Then she saw it: a larger wolf than the one Roger had killed was slinking toward her, its belly flat on the snow. Its left eye was missing; the other glittered with grim purpose.

The wolf charged. Alanna drew Lightning, hoping to spear the huge animal before it leaped. The crust on the snow beneath her broke. She stumbled, Lightning opening a slash in the wolf's side before flying out of her hand. Furious at being wounded, the wolf whirled and charged again.

There was no time to retrieve her sword. Alanna gripped her dagger and, aiming for his blind side, threw herself onto the giant animal's back. Girl and wolf rolled over in the snow, a blur of grey and tan flashing with the white of the wolf's teeth and the copper of Alanna's hair.

Roger looked up; the clearing was ringed with hunters. Myles gripped Jonathan's shoulder, holding the younger man back. The Prince's eyes were terrible with fear for his friend.

Alanna did not see the reinforcements. She saw nothing but the wolf, who was doing his best to fling her off his back. She held on desperately striking again and again with her knife. Suddenly the wolf shuddered and howled; her blade had entered his side. He fell, his paws twitching. She had stabbed him to the heart.

She let Jonathan pull her free of the wolf's body. "Are you insane?" he whispered, hugging her tightly for a moment.

"It attacked me." Alanna pushed Jon away gently, holding the ember-stone for comfort. Suddenly the colors, the sounds, even the smells in the clearing were very sharp. She was startled to see a bright orange glow around Roger. Even more odd was the fact that the same orange fire was fading from the bodies of the two wolves. Alanna looked at them and at Roger, puzzled. What was she seeing? The color of Roger's magic was orange. What had that to do with the wolves?

A huntsman was examining the wolf she had just killed. "'Tis Demon Grey," he told the King positively. "I shot out this eye myself three weeks past. That would be his mate," he added, nodding to the wolf claimed by Roger's spear.

"Are you all right?" Myles asked Alanna, worried by the strange look on her face.

Alanna released the ember-stone. All traces of orange fire, in Roger or in the wolves, was gone. "Am I?" she asked, not thinking about what she said. "I'm not sure."

～

That night Alanna waited until she and Faithful were alone in her room and Jonathan was out at a party before she took the ember-stone from beneath her shirt. The cat watched her, his tail twitching, as she looked around for a suitable object to experiment on. Finally she placed an old shirt in front of the hearth. After putting the stone on a table within reach, she concentrated on the shirt. Reaching toward it, she recited the Spell for Transforming. The spell was a hard one, requiring power and concentration, but she had both in plenty these days. Her weakness of the summer was gone, and the reserves of her Gift were greater than ever. She even wondered if she didn't *enjoy* using magic sometimes.

Purple fire flowed from her fingers into the shirt. It twitched and twisted, its outline slowly straightening and turning brown. Sweat rolled down Alanna's cheeks as she ended the spell. The shirt made a final struggle to stay a shirt before turning into a log of firewood. With a flick of her fingers, Alanna magically threw the log onto the fire. As it crackled and started to burn, she grabbed the ember-stone.

The log, the air between her and the hearth, even her fingertips glowed a brilliant violet. Slowly the color faded, and she put the Goddess's token down, Faithful walked over and rubbed against her legs, meowing, until she bent and picked him up, petting him absently.

"I don't think I've ever held it when magic was being used before," she whispered to the cat. "I always kept it hidden in Roger's class. I was afraid he'd guess something was strange about it. I wonder if it will always show me when there's sorcery around?"

When did you see magic used before? Faithful asked.

"This afternoon," she whispered. "The color of Roger's Gift was on him and the two wolves." She began to pace, still holding her pet. "And what's the answer to that? What could he gain from magicking Demon Grey and his mate?"

Faithful hooked his claws into her tunic and climbed up onto her shoulder, perching there. *Whom did Demon Grey try to kill?*

"Me," Alanna whispered. "He tried to kill me."

∾

$\mathcal{T}$he spring flew by, and Alanna's seventeenth birthday arrived. She rose and dressed before dawn that morning, then made her way to the underground levels and the Chapel of the Ordeal. It was deserted, except for the caretakers; priests came here only during the Midwinter Festival when would-be knights undertook the Ordeal. For two hours she sat and stared at the Chamber's iron door, thinking. *Only a year and a half. Just eighteen months between me and what's in there. It's not enough time!*

Evidently Faithful judged that she had been there long enough. He left her with her thoughts, reappearing with Jonathan on his heels. The Prince took one look at Alanna's white face and dragged her out of the Chapel, closing the door firmly.

"Brooding about it only makes it worse," he told her kindly. "Why think about it all? When the time comes, you'll go in there if you're ready or not. There's nothing you can do to prevent it, so come have some breakfast."

At lunch she received small gifts from Jon, Myles and George, and her friends drank her health. It was hard to believe she'd had six birthdays since coming to the palace. It was hard to believe so much had happened to her.

That night she slipped away early. She was too restless to socialize, and too nervous to sleep. The cause could have been the sight of Jonathan dancing with Lady Delia. From all the signs, the Prince planned to spend the night with the beautiful, green-eyed woman. Alanna didn't want to be there when they left together.

Thinking of Delia sent her to the wooden chest she kept at the foot of her bed, locked and magically protected. Opening it, she drew out her pretty clothes—a lace-trimmed chemise, delicate silk stockings, tiny leather slippers, a purple silk dress. She even took out the black wig she normally wore in public: there weren't enough violet-eyed redheads around to warrant her leaving her rooms without some kind of disguise.

She dressed and admired herself in the mirror. She wasn't a beauty like Delia, but she wasn't a hag, either. Defiantly she picked up a cloak and threw it over her shoulders. There was no law that said she had to be a boy on her seventeenth birthday, and Faithful wasn't there just then to advise caution. Touching the ember-stone and feeling the charm to ward off pregnancy beside it, Alanna grinned. She'd never do anything to get herself pregnant, of that she was certain. Still, she couldn't help but think of…

Amused that she was silly enough to wonder what sex was like, Alanna peered out her door. The hallway was clear, and she was going for a walk in the gardens! What if Jonathan *was* with Delia? She was free and independent, and *that* was the important thing!

She felt bold and wonderful, strolling through

the luxurious palace gardens by herself. Finding an isolated bench, she put her cloak aside and sat down. The moon was full, and she relaxed in its soft silver glow, turning her face up to it. *A night for lovers,* she thought, then bit her lip. She had no lover, and she didn't want one.

She left her cloak and walked through the rose gardens, inhaling the heavy scent of the blooming flowers. From here she could see the long terrace, where she had left Jonathan and Delia. Glancing at it, she could see a man standing there now; he was watching her. Suddenly he went inside, and she lost her spirit of adventure. She didn't want one of her gallant friends coming out here to romance her; life was complicated enough!

He was waiting for her beside the bench where she had left her cloak.

"Hullo," he said casually, holding the garment up. "I think this is yours."

Alanna slid the wig from her hair. "How did you know it was me, Jonathan?"

He came forward, taking one of her hands in his. "I guessed. And then I saw how you walked and I was sure."

Alanna made a face. "Mistress Cooper tries to cure me of walking like a boy, but it doesn't seem to take."

Jonathan lifted the gold charm off her throat, examining it. "What's this?" he asked. His voice was soft and warm.

Alanna was thankful for the darkness that kept him from seeing her blush. "It's a charm to—keep me from having children," she stammered. "Mistress Cooper gave it to me a—a long time ago."

Jon chuckled. "Have you ever tried it out?" he asked, putting his free arm around her. Alanna braced herself against his chest, trying to ignore the silly fluttering in her stomach or the heat running through her body.

"What's *that* supposed to mean?" she asked gruffly.

"This." Swiftly he kissed her again and again. Alanna felt giddy and was grateful that his tight hold kept her from falling. She was scared. She suddenly realized *she* wanted to be the one in his bed tonight.

Jonathan stopped kissing her, only to start unlacing her bodice.

Alanna shoved him away, terrified. "No!" she gasped, grabbing her laces. "I was crazy to think— Jonathan, please!"

The Prince realized she was trembling, her hands shaking too badly for her to lace herself. He shook his head and did the work for her.

"You're fighting what has to be," he said, "and you know it as well as I do."

"I—I know no such thing," she stammered. "I promised myself once that I'd *never* love a man! Maybe I almost broke that promise just now because of moonlight and silliness—"

"Stop it," he told her sternly. He made her look up at him. "We belong to each other. Is that silliness? Surely you've realized all along this had to happen." When she did not answer, he sighed. "Go away, before I change my mind."

Alanna ran. Once inside her room, she bolted the door, undressed and threw her clothes into a corner. This was what came of wearing a dress! Men got ideas when a person wore skirts! *George vowed love to you without ever seeing you in skirts,* a reasonable part of her mind said, but Alanna kicked that thought away. She paced nervously, snapping her fingers. Where was Faithful? She didn't want to be alone when Jonathan came back to his room.

Suddenly her knees weakened, and she sat on the bed. Of course Jonathan wouldn't come back. He'd go to Delia now. He didn't want Alanna; he just wanted a girl to have fun with. *Oh?* said that nasty, reasonable corner of her mind. *Then why did he say what he did? Why did he say you belonged with him?*

Hadn't the Goddess told her to learn to love? Did she love Jonathan?

A sound in the other room startled her. He hadn't gone to Delia! He was preparing for bed in his own room, moving quietly so he wouldn't disturb her. He hadn't been looking just for amusement!

Alanna's lip quivered. She *wanted* Jonathan's

love. To be honest, she had wanted that love for a long time.

She rapped on the door between their rooms. "Jon?"

He opened the door. His eyes were bright as he looked at her. Alanna swallowed. "I'm scared. Help me, please."

Jonathan's voice was rough as he said, "I'm scared, too. At least we can be scared together."

eight

Fears

*A*lanna was happy that summer. During the day she had lessons and duties—fewer lessons now and more duties, because she was entering her last year as a squire. She had Myles to advise her when Coram wrote with a particularly difficult problem at Trebond. She went to Mistress Cooper to talk and to learn more about a woman's life. At night, Jonathan taught her about loving. She was sorry to see the leaves begin to change color: somehow she knew her quiet, happy time was not going to last much longer.

*D*elia of Eldorne paced in front of Duke Roger's chair, her green eyes glinting with anger. "I don't understand it!" she snapped for the tenth time. "I had him *here*—" She held out a slender white hand, palm up, before clenching it into a fist. "And now I suppose I'm to consider myself privileged if he dances with me *once* at a party!" She threw herself to her knees in front of Roger's chair, looking up at him prettily. "Master, forgive me," she begged.

"I did everything you told me to. He just—" She stopped and looked downward, fluttering her heavy lashes.

Roger smiled and reached out, stroking her flowing, dark hair. "Don't fret, pretty one," he told her. "That young man is proving very slippery indeed. Fortunately, I have other plans ready to be put into action."

"Other plans?" Delia breathed, her eyes wide. "Master, can I help? Can I do anything to assist you? Only tell me!"

Roger looked off into the distance, still stroking the kneeling girl's hair. "There is nothing you can do for me just now," he remarked absently. "The next move on the board is mine." He looked down at her again, his eyes unreadable. "But you must hold yourself ready. If all goes wrong, I will need your help more than ever."

"Nothing could go wrong!" Delia protested violently. "Not when *you* have planned it!"

Duke Roger of Conté smiled again. "Perhaps you are right, my dear," he remarked. "I hope so. In the meantime, be a good child and wait. Give Jonathan to understand that, while *he* is no longer attentive to you, *your* affections remain his."

"And your other plans?" Delia whispered.

The sorcerer tugged his beard. "You will see," he promised her. "I cannot move carelessly—not yet—but I think you know me well enough to be able to detect what I am doing." He laughed outright. "No one *else* will be able to—I've made sure of that!"

～

*A*nd in October a fever went through the Eastern Lands, as sicknesses often did. Few died, although many were ill, and the Queen was one of the sickest. Lianne had never been strong, and the fever refused to give her up easily. She recovered at last, but she did not get completely well.

During the Queen's illness Alanna and Jonathan were separated for the first time since Alanna's birthday, as Jonathan sat vigil by his mother's bedside day and night. Their love affair was not the same after that—Jon was too worried about his mother's health. He was not the only one. Alanna did not like to see the Queen picking at her food and losing weight she did not have to lose. Lianne also developed a cough that refused to go away, despite Duke Baird's best care.

"Myles," Alanna began one December night as they were playing chess, "does the Queen's weakness look—*right* to you?"

"It looks like it's killing her." Myles frowned. "Is that supposed to look 'right' to me?"

Alanna examined a knight thoughtfully. "Duke Baird's the finest healer in Tortall. Why can't he help the Queen?"

Myles looked sharply at her. "This isn't just idle conversation, is it? What's bothering you?"

Alanna nibbled her thumbnail. "I don't like it," she admitted. "I saw how much Duke Baird can do at the Drell. He's blessed by the gods. A fever, a cough—Duke Baird can heal those things in a moment. But now he can't. The only other time I saw him this helpless was during the Sweating Sickness." She moved a pawn forward one square. "There are some people who think the Sweating Sickness was caused by a sorcerer. You were one of them, remember?"

"Do you think there's a connection?" Myles asked.

"I don't know what to think," Alanna replied. Then she nodded her head. "Yes, I do, and I'm going to say it. Too many bad things happen to Jonathan or to people close to him. I think—"

"Alan, the Queen was never very strong," Myles reminded her. "The Sweating Sickness ruined her health. Her weakness now is probably natural. Think carefully before you make any accusations, please." Myles drew a deep breath.

"The enemy you will make is too powerful for you to accuse without evidence—and plenty of it."

Alanna looked Myles in the eye. "You suspect him, too."

Myles sighed and tugged his beard. "I have no *proof*, Alan. He's too clever to be easily caught. All I have—all *you* have—is coincidence. You cannot accuse a man of high treason on coincidence."

"Demon Grey and his mate weren't coincidences." After weeks of wrestling with herself on the matter, Alanna told her friend about discovering that her token could show her when sorcery had been used. She even let Myles hold it. He examined it briefly and returned it to her.

"How did you get this?"

Alanna told him about that meeting in the forest, omitting only that the Goddess had spoken to her as a girl. Men were sometimes chosen by the Mother, and she couldn't bring herself to tell Myles she had lied about her identity for years. The knight listened, his face expressionless. When she finished, he asked, "Is there anything else you think I should know?"

After keeping her suspicions bottled up for so long, Alanna let them spill out. "Duke Gareth's horse had a bur fixed in its saddle blanket when it threw the Duke. And the man who saddled the horse disappeared that same day. The night I was kidnapped by the Tusaine? I talked with Duke Roger. He wanted me to be his friend. He said if I was his friend, I'd live to a ripe old age. I told him I wanted my friends to have the same, and I didn't think that was what *he* wanted. He left, and the fog came up. You remember the fog and that Faithful couldn't be wakened? Isn't it strange that everything happened after he visited me and that the one being that could've helped me—my cat—was knocked out magically? The Tusaines were ready for me, Myles. They used special chains on me. Not only that, but they had *heard* about me, and I wasn't to be released. Who told them so much about me? Jem—Jemis? I don't think he knew I had anything more than a healing Gift. And didn't you ever wonder why the first *major* attack launched by the enemy separated Jonathan from all the others?"

"You have no proof," Myles replied steadily.

"Duke Roger isn't a careless man," Alanna said bitterly. "I have only what I've seen and what I think." She got up and poked the fire, her jaw tight with anger.

"You hate Roger, don't you?" Myles asked quietly. He poured them each a glass of wine.

Alanna paused, thinking. "If hate is wanting to crush someone because you *know* they're evil, then yes—I hate the Duke of Conté."

Myles grasped her by the shoulders. "Be careful. He's too powerful to anger. *You* could easily be the one to die, and no one would know he was to blame. He can do it. You know he can. And if you're out of the way, who will keep him away from Jonathan? He's afraid of you, or he wouldn't have risked exposure to make a friend out of you."

Alanna grinned. Myles had just given her an idea. "I think I know someone else he might fear."

∽

"*D*on't be such a ninny," Alex urged as Alanna struggled with the skates. "Surely you ice-skated at Trebond."

"Not since I was little," Alanna replied curtly,

eyeing the frozen surface before her. Gary and Raoul were racing their squires while Jonathan helped Cythera of Elden to her feet. Another of the Queen's ladies, Gwynnen, was laughing merrily as she performed figure eights under the January sun.

How had she let herself walk into a stupid bet with Alex? She hadn't ice-skated since the time she fell in when she was just five. But everyone had called her chicken, and Jonathan had looked at her with "Please?" in his eyes, and Alex had bet her ten gold nobles she couldn't get around the pond once without falling. Her noble's pride couldn't refuse such a challenge, even though she had been wary of Alex ever since the mock duel when he had nearly killed her.

Her friends applauded as she tottered out onto the ice, Faithful yowling encouragement from the land. He had insisted on coming, although—like any sane cat—he hated water, frozen or not. Alanna tried a few steps, relieved to find the ice was firm beneath her. Getting a little bolder, she skated several feet, stopping only to retie a skate lace.

Without warning Geoffrey and Sacherell swept up behind her and seized her by both arms, taking off with her down the pond's length. Alanna laughed and ordered them to let her go, knowing they wouldn't drop her. Raoul's squire was the best skater in the palace, and Geoffrey was quite good for someone born and reared in Persopolis. Grinning, they deposited her in front of Alex.

"Well?" The young knight grinned, pointing to the ice. "A bet's a bet!"

Alanna set off doggedly around the edge of the pond, her legs pumping steadily. Once she got into the rhythm of it, she had only to watch for bumps and rough spots in the ice. *This is more fun than I remembered,* she thought, reaching the far end of the pond, many yards away from her friends. *Perhaps I should skate more!*

At this end of the pond there were several clumps of reeds. She gave them a wide berth, remembering that ice was weaker in such areas. Only a third of the way remained to go when the ice gave way beneath her. She fell into bone-cold water like a stone, biting back a scream of fright. It had happened just this way when she was five, with the skates pulling her down. She fought to get them off her feet, holding her breath and cursing the fear of cold that made her wear so many clothes. There! The skates were off her feet, and she was plowing toward the surface again. Her lungs were bursting. Terror rose up, choking her. She forced herself to think, knowing that if she panicked now she would be dead. Surely the air was just above her...

Her hands contacted ice. She groped, trying to find the hole through which she had come; but it was useless. Shivering helplessly in the water, she felt for the ember-stone. She didn't even realize it was in her numb hand until its fire blazed out and a hole melted in the ice above her head. She shot to the surface, inhaling a huge gasp of air, before her sodden clothes pulled her under.

Once more, she thought grimly, and she forced herself to the surface again. This time strong hands gripped both her arms, and Jon and Raoul pulled her out onto the ice. "Did someone go for help?" Jonathan asked tensely as he pulled off her jacket. "Get he—get his outer things off!"

"The girls went," Gary replied, tugging off Alanna's mittens. "Mithros, Alan, you gave us a— Faithful, get away from there!"

Alanna tried to turn her head. "What's he doing?" she gasped.

Raoul frowned as he tugged off her remaining boot. "He's licking the ice. C'mon, Alan, let's get you onto dry land."

Alanna enjoyed the unique sensation of being carried by someone who handled her as if she were a kitten. "Licking the ice?" she asked sleepily.

"I'll be right there," Jonathan said. He and Alex skated over to the cat. "Come on, Faithful," he instructed sternly. "You'll worry Alan."

Alex was shaking his head. "I don't understand. This pond's been frozen solid for weeks. How—"

"Why do animals lick ice?" Jon asked, his voice odd. Carefully he knelt beside Faithful, keeping an eye on the wide hole in the ice where Alanna had gone through. He rubbed his ungloved hand near the hole and tasted. "Someone threw salt on this part of the ice," he announced slowly.

"Look how it's pitted and marked right here."

"Murder," Alex whispered, looking more closely. "But which of us is a murderer's target? Could it be just a very bad idea of a joke?"

"I'm not laughing," Jonathan commented dryly. "Are you?"

∽

Once she had recovered from her icy dunking, Alanna decided to take action. She sent a verbal message, not daring to trust her thoughts to a letter, to Thom through George. She needed her brother's help. Only Roger could have been behind the mishap on the duckpond, and she knew she wanted no more such "mishaps" happening to her. She also found it interesting that Alex had been there.

Weeks went by without an answer and without the messenger's return. George finally sent out search parties, and in March Alanna had an answer—of sorts.

"My messenger was slain," George told her. "Five arrows in his back, all poisoned. Someone was takin' no chances."

Alanna frowned. "I'll have to go myself," she said worriedly. "Not now, the mountain passes are snowed in. And Jonathan needs me."

George forced her to look at him. "You're in love with Jon, aren't you?" he asked softly. "And me a blind fool not to have seen it before."

Alanna shook him off. "I don't know what love

is," she said uncomfortably. "At least, not the kind *you're* talking about—the forever kind."

George laughed and shook his head. "Lass, when will you learn to see what's before your nose?"

Alanna reached up and tweaked George's own nose. "When I have something to see," she teased. "So stop trying to make me see something that isn't there."

George smiled. "You're a stubborn youngling," he told her. "It's one of your charms. And if you're plannin' any ride to the City of the Gods, I'm goin' with you." He silenced her protest by putting a large hand over her mouth. "Didn't you hear me before? Five poison-tipped arrows in my man, and it's as well for you he carried a message rather than a letter. He was searched, his things spread all over the snow. It's good we've had a cold winter—everything was frozen just as it was when they killed him. So, miss, like it or no, I go with you when you visit your brother."

Alanna made a face and kept quiet. When the time came, she would get away without George. She could take care of herself!

ᴄ◡

Jonathan did not want her to go, but Alanna rode for the City of the Gods in early April, leaving Faithful with strict instructions to watch the Prince and to get Myles if anything happened. Saddling

Moonlight before dawn, she slipped out of the palace. Few people—no rogues—were about in the city. She thought she had fooled George, since she had given no one more than half a day's warning of her departure. She was wrong. The thief was waiting for her at the gates, dressed for riding and mounted on a sturdy bay.

"Jonathan told you," Alanna accused her friend.

"No. Stefan keeps messenger-birds. I've got you under tight watch, youngling, and it's well for you that I do."

Since there was nothing she could do, Alanna laughed and fell in beside George. Would she ever be able to outwit him?

The ride north was a good one. George was witty and entertaining; he had some wonderful stories to tell. They stopped at Trebond for a night. Coram was shocked to see the company Alanna kept and read her a strong lecture, but Alanna shrugged it off. Instead she spent time with the young man Coram was training as his replacement; he was a nice fellow, with a small family and some education. Alanna knew when she was done talking to him that he would serve her as faithfully as Coram did. Plans were made for Coram to come to the palace in November, in order to be there when Alanna underwent the Ordeal.

Alanna and George rode on to the City of the Gods. Alanna sighed wearily when they finally arrived before the City's great walls. Grey mountains bare of almost any greenery stretched for leagues around, making for a dull, tiring ride.

"How can Thom live in such a cursed ugly place?" she asked George. "I'd go mad if I had to look at this all the time."

"He probably doesn't notice," her friend replied. "Most scholars don't."

The warrior-priests who manned the gates showed them to the Mithran Cloisters. As they passed the Convent of the Mother of Mountains, Alanna shuddered. She had almost spent six years behind those walls. Now, more than ever, she appreciated her escape!

An orange-robed initiate admitted them to the Cloisters; novices took their horses. An ancient yellow man in the black-and-gold robes of a master tottered out to greet them. "We are honored to have you among us, Squire Alan, Freeman Cooper," he said. "I am Si-cham, Chief of the Masters here."

Alanna bowed very low; as a sorcerer, Si-cham would be nearly as powerful as Duke Roger. As a priest, he was the head of the Cult of Mithros for all the Eastern Lands. "We would be honored if you would join us for our evening meal," this friendly old man went on. "We get little news of the world."

"We'd be honored to come," George said.

"Excellent, excellent. Follow me, if you please. I do not believe Adept Thom is expecting you?"

Alanna smiled grimly. "I wanted to surprise him."

Si-cham looked sharply at her before knocking on one of the many doors lining a long hallway. "Do you think much surprises Adept Thom?"

Before Alanna could answer such an astonishing question, Thom opened the door. He was bearded, taller—older. He hugged Alanna with enthusiasm, crying, "Brother Dear!" Seeing Alanna's companion, Thom widened his violet eyes. "Not—George Cooper?" He grinned.

"The same," George replied, extending his hand. "I've heard a thing or two about you myself."

"Surely some of it was good," Thom quipped, shaking the offered hand. He looked at Master Si-cham as Alanna dazedly realized, *He knew we were coming. He wasn't surprised at all.*

"Their things have been taken to the guest's wing." The Master's voice, warm and friendly a moment ago, was suddenly chilly. "And they have accepted an invitation to take the evening meal with us."

Thom lifted a single coppery eyebrow. "Oh?" he asked, his voice too sweet. "Then I will have to join you—won't I?"

"It will be a change." The old man's voice was as dry as autumn leaves. "I will leave you to talk now." He hurried away down the long hall.

Alanna was confused. "I don't get it. He was very friendly a moment ago."

"They've been angry with me ever since I

stopped playing the idiot and passed the written examinations for Mastery. Come in; sit down. Wine?" Thom rang a bell, and a servant in the white robe of a novice came in. He gave the boy orders, pretending not to notice that Alanna and George were staring at him. When the novice was gone, Alanna sat down hard. Most would-be Masters did not even try for that title until they were at least thirty.

"You passed the written examinations for *Mastery?*" Her voice emerged from her throat in a squeak.

"Two weeks ago. It was easier than you think." Thom shrugged, motioning George to take the chair beside Alanna while he sat in the third. "All that's left are the spoken examinations and the Ordeal of Sorcery."

"You call that *all?*" Alanna demanded weakly.

Thom laughed at her shock. "I was ready for this more than a year ago. And now they can't wait for me to finish and get out of here. I make them nervous."

The wine came. Alanna drank hers in one gulp and poured another glass while George told Thom about their ride to the City of the Gods. When Alanna was calmer, Thom turned back to her.

"Now. What brings you two to me the moment the passes are clear? Or rather, sister, what brings *you?* I believe I guess correctly when I say George came to protect you."

George smiled and sipped his wine. "Truth to tell, I came for the ride. Surely you know that Alanna can take care of herself."

Thom smiled cruelly. "You came to protect her from a certain smiling gentleman," he said. "Or did you think I had forgotten him? He hasn't forgotten *me*. There are two people watching me here."

"It's just as well you're getting your Mastery, then, isn't it?" Alanna shrugged. If Thom could be matter-of-fact about it, so could she. "I need you at the palace."

"Do you indeed?"

"Don't take that arch tone with me, brother," she said tartly. "I used to duck you in the fishpond. I'll try to do it again if you make me angry. This is too important."

Thom laughed. "So serious! All right, what's the problem?"

They talked until the bells called them to the evening meal, and then they talked again until very late. Alanna wanted Thom in the palace to watch over Jonathan when she left. Thom did not refuse; he wanted to live well at Court for a while. With the most important question settled, Alanna and George told Thom everything they knew or suspected about Duke Roger. Alanna had the only surprise for either man as she explained about the ember-stone. She finished telling her brother about the tests she had performed on the charm and sat back, yawning tiredly. She could remember the watch had called midnight, but that had been at least an hour ago.

George shook his head, smiling ruefully. "Have you any more surprises for me, then?" he asked gently.

"Don't be silly," she replied. "I would've told you before, but the time was never right. It's not something I think I should talk much about."

Thom stood and looked down at her. "One of the gods themselves," he remarked softly. "What I wouldn't give to have been there with you."

"I wish you *had* been with me," Alanna said frankly. "I was scared to death. Except maybe she wouldn't have talked to me if you'd been there."

Thom stretched out his hand. "Let me see it."

Her eyes on her twin's, Alanna slowly pulled the chain over her head. The ember-stone swung in the air, its inner fire burning. Thom took it, holding it up before his eyes. "Does the glow give you away at night?" he asked absent-mindedly. Alanna could see his mind wasn't on her, but on the problems and questions posed by the Goddess's token. This was Thom's other face, his scholar's face, the one he wore when he was tracking down some ancient spell in rotting scrolls and half-burned books.

"No," she replied, feeling a little forlorn. This was a place her twin went where she couldn't follow. "It burns inside, but it doesn't burn, if you know what I mean."

George, seeing the loneliness on her face, stood

behind her, rubbing her shoulders. She smiled up at him gratefully. Was there anything that George didn't understand about her?

"Fascinating," Thom whispered. Suddenly his face tightened. He threw the charm into the air and pointed at it, shouting a word neither Alanna nor George knew. There was a great, soundless explosion. The room rocked, and Alanna grabbed George to keep him from falling. All around the Cloisters, lamps flared up and men shouted questions. Alanna glared at Thom. Shrugging, her brother handed back the ember-stone. The chain was gone; a small bead of molten gold clung to the stone's crystal exterior. "No damage," Thom reassured her.

Alanna got her wind back. "No damage!" she yelled furiously. "*What did you do to it?*"

"He used a word of Command," said a dry voice from the doorway. Si-cham, wearing a crumpled dressing gown over his sleeping robe, stood there. "Is the thing of immortal origin?"

Wordlessly Alanna handed the ember-stone over, mentally promising to get Thom for putting her in this position. The yellow man examined the stone for a moment before handing it back. "He Commanded it to give up its secrets," the Master explained. "Only a thing made by the immortals could resist such a Command, as I see this has. You shouldn't give your brother such dangerous toys to play with, Squire Alan." Si-cham glanced at Thom. "I suppose you realize you've disrupted a number of very delicate spells some of the Masters have been working on. It will take many of them weeks to repair the damage."

Thom shrugged. "It was necessary," he said coolly. "I had to learn how powerful it was."

"I see." Si-cham's smile was small and grim. "Very well. To teach you the virtues of *warning* your fellow scholars when you are about to play with the basic forces of Nature, your Ordeal of Sorcery shall be to set to rights the work you destroyed tonight." The ancient Master nodded to Alanna. "Until tomorrow morning, Squire Alan."

Alanna turned to her brother when the door closed behind Si-cham. "Couldn't you make friends with them?" she wanted to know. "I like Master Si-cham. And the others—"

Thom shook his head. "They're afraid of me because I'm better than they are. They'd hate me even if I went out of my way to be *good* to them; and I'm certainly not going to do that."

Alanna frowned, worried. "You're going to be very lonely," she said frankly.

Thom laughed. "I have the Gift. That's enough for me."

"I wonder. It doesn't seem as if it would be enough." She remembered what the Goddess had said about learning to love. Thom would have a lonely life without love or friendship. She at least had friends. Was it possible she had learned to love, as well?

They spent another day in the Cloisters, talking to others while Thom studied and conferring further with Thom. When Alanna and George left at dawn the next day, Alanna knew that her powerful brother would soon come to help her protect Jonathan. That at least she looked to; it would take a great burden off her shoulders.

They rode for half a day in silence, Alanna thinking about Thom. George waited to break the silence until they halted for the noon meal.

"Your brother is an interestin' fellow."

Alanna laughed shortly. "That he is."

"He'll be powerful protection for Jon. You can go adventurin' without another thought." Alanna nodded. George watched her for a moment before adding, "Was he always so proud?"

Alanna raised miserable eyes to her friend. "I don't know," she admitted. "I don't *think* so. He was different when we went home to bury our father. I could see then he was turning hard. I suppose that as powerful as he is, he has every right to be proud. Not everyone can harness so much magic. I never tried; I was afraid to."

"A wise kind of fear," George pointed out. "Besides, what would you be—a fine warrior *and* a great sorcerer?"

"It's not that," Alanna protested, realizing George thought she might be a little jealous. "It's that he seems so *lonely*. And he doesn't even realize it."

George raised his eyebrows. "Do I believe my ears? Alanna the Heartless talkin' *for* love instead of against it?"

"Don't tease, George. He's my brother. *I* love him."

"He knows that," George said, hugging her around the shoulders. "And I know I for one envy him. Now, eat up. We've a long ride home."

❦

*T*his time they did not stop at Trebond. They rode past Trebond Way, Alanna stopping only for a moment to look toward her home. More and more the palace felt like home to her, and Trebond was only a place on the map.

It was sunset the day after they passed Trebond, and they still had a few leagues to go before reaching the next wayhouse. It was George who sensed trouble, pulling his bay up short. His nostrils flared, as if he were sniffing the wind.

"Unless my city-bred nose betrays me—" He broke off with a cry of pain: an ugly black arrow sprouted from his collarbone. Men were pouring out of the trees, surrounding them. "Ride on!" cried George between gritted teeth.

Moonlight reared, flailing with her hooves at the two ruffians who tried to grab her reins. George yanked a dagger from its sheath and hurled it into a man's throat. "Ride!" he yelled as four more swarmed down upon them.

"No!" Alanna cried fiercely. She rode Moonlight straight at a man who was putting an arrow to his bow. The mare trampled him ruthlessly as Alanna drew Lightning, slashing at a third attacker. George drew his own sword to kill the man who was trying to pull him from his saddle. His face was pale, and Alanna remembered with horror that the first messenger to Thom had been slain with poisoned arrows. With a yell of fury she cut down two men who were trying to herd her away from George. Wheeling Moonlight, she saw George fling his second dagger into an attacker's shoulder.

George pulled his bay to a halt, his face white in the gathering darkness. "Never mind me," he gasped, "the arrow's not poisoned. Find out from that one what you can!" He pointed to the man he had just wounded, the only attacker still standing.

Alanna cut the killer off as he tried to run, kicking him down before she dismounted. Furious, she leveled her sword at the man's throat. He stared at her, trying to inch away.

"Hold still!" Alanna yelled, her voice cracking with rage. This animal and his friends had hurt George! "Who sent you? Who!"

"*You* weren't to be hurt," the ruffian babbled, his eyes wide with terror. "'I want the boy alive,' we was told, and him never sayin' you was a killer, and the man, too! 'They'll be easy game. Jest bring the

boy an' kill the man an' there's gold in it for you.'
That's what we was told—"

"*Who* told you?" Alanna roared.

The man opened his mouth and tried to speak.
He made little choking noises as large beads of
sweat rolled off his face. Suddenly he turned pale
and screamed, clawing at invisible hands on his
throat. His eyes rolled up and he collapsed—dead.
Quickly Alanna fumbled for the ember-stone under
her clothing. She gripped it, and instantly saw
traces of orange fire vanishing from the man's
body.

"Sorcery," she whispered. She turned to look at
George. Her friend was swaying in his saddle. There
was no time to waste. Alanna grabbed a length of
rope from her saddlebags and tied George to his
horse's back. Mounting Moonlight, she gave the
man her brandy flask while she examined the
wound. The shaft had passed through the muscle of
George's shoulder; the arrowhead stood clear of his
back. Steeling herself, Alanna cut the arrow feathers
away and pulled the shaft through the wound. The
thief fainted against her as she worked, and she
could only be thankful. Leaning George forward on
his horse, Alanna took the other animal's reins and
set off into the night.

It seemed like forever came and went before
they reached the wayhouse. Once there, Alanna
snapped orders to the hostlers, watching anxiously
as they drew George off his horse's back and carried
him inside. She brushed aside the innwife's offer to

send for a healer, explaining briefly that she was a healer herself. A room was quickly prepared for them, and a maid fetched brandy, boiling water and clean linen for bandages. Alanna worked to clean and bind up the wound, putting her most powerful healing magic on it. Then, exhausted by the fight and the magic, she watched George late into the night. She didn't like his color. He'd lost so much blood...

"Don't die on me," she whispered when the clock struck midnight and he still had not moved. "It's only a little shoulder wound. Goddess, George—don't die on me."

His eyes flickered open and he smiled. "I didn't know you cared," he whispered. "And why insult me? I won't die for a wee nick like this; I've had worse in my day."

Alanna wiped her wet cheeks. "Of course I care, you unprincipled pickpocket!" she whispered. "Of course I care."

∽

*F*aithful woke Alanna shortly after dawn on her eighteenth birthday. *Wake up and get dressed*, the cat told her. *You don't want the surprise they've planned to be a surprise for them as well as for you. Jonathan says to hurry!*

Alanna was tucking her shirt into her breeches when the Prince rapped on her door. "Are you decent, Squire?" he demanded.

Alanna yanked the door open. "I'm always

decent, overlord," she replied. Then she saw that Gary, Raoul and Alex were with him. "Isn't it a little early for this?" she asked plaintively.

The filed into her room, each carrying a bulky package.

"That's all right, grouch," Gary said, thumping her shoulder. "Happy birthday."

The young men piled their packages onto the bed; then they turned to look at Jonathan. He glared back at them. "I thought *Raoul* was going to tell Alan."

"You talk better than I do," Raoul said.

"What they're trying *not* to tell you," Gary said patiently, "is that we discussed it, and we decided our hero-to-be should be properly outfitted." He gestured to the packages on the bed. "The gifts are from all of us, and Their Majesties, and my father, uh—Duke Baird, Douglass, Geoffrey, Sacherell— did I forget anyone?"

"I don't think so," Alex said.

"Myles said he was damned if he would get up at this hour, but if you went to the stables, you'd find something from him," Raoul added.

Jonathan handed Alanna the largest, heaviest package, "Go on," he urged when she simply stared at it. "It's for you."

The package contained the lightest mail shirt Alanna had ever handled, washed with gold. The other packages held a gold-washed helmet, a belt made of gold wire picked out with amethysts, soft kid riding gloves, a gold-trimmed sheath for Lightning and a matching dagger, and gold-washed mail leggings to match the shirt. Alanna opened all of the gifts silently. The smallest package, from her "Cousin George," contained a black opal ring set in pale gold.

She looked at them, awed and frightened by this show of affection. "I—I don't know what to say."

"Don't say anything," Jonathan advised. "Go take a look at Moonlight."

Myles's gift was a complete outfitting for the mare, made of well-worked leather trimmed with gold. Moonlight voiced her pleasure with a high-pitched whinny, while Faithful sat in a special cup for him attached to the saddle, purring with contentment. Alanna had to cry with happiness, but she hid her face in Moonlight's mane. No one noticed.

No one would accept her thanks, either. The other young men ordered her to be quiet, or, if she *had* to express appreciation, to do so by teaching them the words to the bawdy songs she had learned from the men of Fort Drell.

"Why are you so confused?" Jonathan asked her late that night. "Can't you see we all love you and want you to succeed—even if you insist on leaving us?"

"They'll hate me more than ever when they find out the truth," Alanna said miserably.

"Nonsense. And haven't you thought that some of them may have guessed by now?"

Alanna looked at her friend and lover. "Myles," she whispered. "I'll bet he knows."

Jonathan decided not to say anything about the very odd conversation he had had with Myles the day after the Tusaine kidnapped Alanna. "Why not ask him?" he replied instead.

Alanna was thinking about this when she remembered something else. "Jonathan, I have to have two knights to instruct me in the Code of Chivalry while I take the purifying bath, before the Ordeal. What am I going to do?"

"I suggest you tell Cousin Gary." Jonathan yawned, falling onto his bed. "He'll think it's a wonderful joke. And I think we can instruct you in the Code *after* you bathe."

Alanna grinned, lying down beside him. "You just don't want Gary to see me bare."

"You're right, I don't! Do *you?*" Jonathan asked suspiciously, looking her in the eyes. When Alanna only giggled, Jonathan repeated, "*Do* you?"

"You're very jealous for someone who isn't serious about me." She grinned.

Jonathan made her look at him. "I *am* serious, in my way," he said quietly. "But if I talked of love to you, you'd run off."

"Don't, Jonathan, please," she whispered.

"See what I mean?" He yawned again. "Relax. I certainly can't talk about marriage in any case—"

"I don't want to talk about marriage!" she cried. "I don't want to talk about love, ei—"

Jonathan silenced her with a hand over her mouth. "I love you, Alanna," he said firmly. "Ignore it if you want, but I do love you." He pulled the covers over them. "Now go to sleep."

Alanna lay awake for a long time, wishing he hadn't said it, and glad that he had. She was going away when she became a knight. Nothing could change that. He would have to make a marriage that would be good for the kingdom. Nothing could change *that*, either. And yet—

She thought he was asleep. "I love you, Jonathan," she whispered.

A long arm snaked around her, and he pulled her against his side. "I know," he said "I just wanted to be sure you knew it, too."

nine
❧
The Ordeal

Soon after her birthday, Alanna and Gary went for a day's ride in the Royal Forest. Jonathan watched them leave, knowing what Alanna wanted to discuss with his big cousin. He was nervous, and he wondered how Alanna, with so much more at stake, felt.

"Whatever's on your mind, you may as well say it now and get it over with," Gary advised after they had been riding in silence for an hour. "It must be pretty important."

Alanna wiped a sprinkling of sweat off her upper lip. "It is," she admitted. "Gary, has it—has it ever occurred to you that I might not be the person I *seem* to be?"

He shrugged. "I know you've had a big secret ever since I first met you," he admitted. "I always figured you'd tell me what it was, eventually."

Alanna drew a deep breath. "I'm a girl," she said bluntly. "My—my real name is Alanna. I come from Trebond, and Lord Thom really is my twin brother."

Gary drew his horse up abruptly, staring at her. "That's not funny!"

Alanna drew her gaze off the back of Moonlight's neck, where she had fixed it. "Of course it's not funny; it's the truth!"

"Where are your breasts?" he demanded.

Alanna blushed. "I bind them flat with a special corset I wear."

"But when you bathe—" Gary stopped and whistled. "None of us have ever seen you bathe. Or swim, for that matter!"

"That's right."

Gary tugged his mustache, deep in thought. "Who else knows?" he asked softly.

Alanna swallowed hard. He didn't *seem* to be angry. "Jonathan. George and Mistress Cooper. Coram, my brother Thom. The healing woman at Trebond. Faithful." She petted the cat riding in his special cup on Moonlight's saddle.

For several long moments she could only hear the birds and the forest animals around them. Gary's face was unreadable, but knowing him as she did, she guessed he was putting together all the odds and ends that had puzzled him about her through the years. Suddenly a broad smile broke across Gary's face, and his eyes crinkled up with merriment. "Oh, I can't wait to see their faces!" he whooped as he burst into laughter.

"Anyone in particular?" Alanna wanted to know, puzzled by his amusement. Jonathan had *said* Gary would react this way, but it hadn't seemed possible to her.

"Everyone," the knight gasped, wiping his

streaming eyes. "Just—everyone!"

He continued to laugh as they rode and talked, Alanna explaining everything to him (with the exception of the love she shared with Jonathan). He was amused and delighted about all of it, and happy to be involved.

"Of course I'll instruct when you take the Sacramental Bath. I'd be insulted if you asked anyone else," he informed her over their picnic lunch. "Wait a minute! Your squire—have you picked anyone?"

Alanna shook her head. "I talked it over with your father, and he agreed that it would be a waste of time for me to pick someone when I plan to leave right after Midwinter."

"Right after you tell them who you are, you mean."

Alanna nodded. "A squire couldn't go with me in any case, even if the truth weren't to come out."

Gary cocked an eyebrow at her. "Surely you don't think they'll be glad to be rid of you when they find out the truth."

"Won't they?"

Duke Gareth's son was no fool. "Some will," he said finally. "Those who don't know you well almost certainly will feel that way. But your friends? I think you're being too harsh on them." He sprang up, helping her pack their saddlebags once again. "Oh, I can't wait!"

Jon was relieved, and jealous, when he saw

Alanna and Gary that night at dinner, smiling and relaxed. They quickly told him what happened. It gave all three of them something to talk about—and laugh over in secret—during the long summer. Those talks were good for Alanna. So used to seeing her masquerade as a life-or-death matter, she had never learned to laugh about it. Gary, Jonathan and George proceeded to teach her, and she gathered new insights about what she had done and about those closest to her from them. Somehow the prospect of telling the truth seemed less terrifying as a result.

To everyone who knew her, Alanna seemed to change in the months between her eighteenth birthday and Midwinter Festival. She was still attentive in her classes, performing her duties perfectly, but it was obvious her thoughts were elsewhere. She often sneaked into the city in disguise, going to the Temple of the Great Mother Goddess to meditate. She had a good many things to ponder—Jon, George, Thom, Duke Roger, the proper time to tell the King and Queen the truth—but chief on her mind was the iron door of the Chamber of the Ordeal. What she feared there, or why, she was never quite certain. She only knew that for the first time in her life she wished she could grab time and hold on to it, keeping it from going forward. Even the thought that she might pass the Ordeal and leave on her adventures gave her no pleasure. She had learned to love the palace and the people who lived there and she knew she would miss them. In fact, she was no longer positive she wanted to go.

"So don't leave," Myles advised when she mentioned it to him. "Most young knights fight in the service of the Realm after they get their shields. Certainly Duke Gareth and His Majesty will be more than happy to have you stay."

Alanna shook her head. The only thing she still looked forward to was the relief of telling everyone who she was.

She got up and hugged her shaggy friend impulsively. "I love you, Myles," she whispered, blinking back tears. "I'll come back often, I promise."

Myles patted her back gently and offered her his handkerchief. "I know you will. I may not know much, but that I *do* know."

∾

George watched her pace his chambers, his hazel eyes unreadable. "You're only wearin' yourself out," he pointed out practically. "How will you be stayin' awake all night if you tire yourself in the afternoon?"

Alanna wiped her hand over her sweating face. "I don't think I've ever been this scared in my life, George."

"Not when you fought the Ysandir? Or when you almost drowned while skating?" She shook her head, fingering the ember at her throat. "Not when you faced Dain, or the Tusaine knights attackin' you?"

"No. Don't you see? I could *fight* them. Dealing with something I can't see, something I know nothing about—" Alanna boosted Faithful up to her shoulder and went over to the window, staring out at the city. "I can't do anything except let it happen. That—that isn't the way I do things, George. You of all people should know that."

"Here." The thief pressed a glass of brandy into her hand, sipping from one he had poured himself. "I've been keepin' this bottle by special. And what's more special than now, the day before your Ordeal? Drink up, lass."

Alanna obeyed, savoring the brandy's rich taste. "This is really good!" she approved. "Normally I just drink this stuff to clear my head, but—this is quite pleasant. You didn't steal it, did you?" she demanded, as suspicious as ever.

Faithful jumped down from her shoulder as George laughed outright. "Would I serve you or Jon stolen goods?" he asked. "No, don't answer me. Look. There's the tax stamp on it, as clear as day. Vintages like this are better than gold, and better watched."

Alanna yawned. "It's not that I don't trust you, George." She yawned again, and again. "So sleepy…" She looked at her friend through rapidly closing eyes. "You—you drugged it!" she accused.

George caught her as she sagged, her eyelids fluttering shut. "Did you really think I'd let you fret yourself sick, with such an important night ahead of you?" he asked softly. Alanna muttered and stirred, sound asleep. George scooped her up and carried her into his bedroom, placing her gently on his bed. "You knew," he commented to Faithful as the cat leaped up beside Alanna. "Why didn't you warn her I was puttin' a little extra in the brandy?"

The cat switched his tail. *Cover her up well,* he advised George. *She gets cold easily.*

The thief laughed and obeyed before joining Gary, Raoul and Jonathan downstairs.

∽

George returned Alanna to the palace just after sunset, where the ritual of Midwinter and of the Ordeal caught her up at last, leaving her only enough time to worry about doing everything properly. She ate lightly; if Myles hadn't stood over her for every bite, she would have eaten nothing at all. Then she changed into the white garments she would wear in the Chamber of the Ordeal. Shortly after the eighth hour was cried, Jonathan and Gary came to escort her to the baths.

As Alanna splashed in the unheated water, her friends waited in a nearby chamber, talking quietly.

"I wish this was over," Jonathan announced, listening to Alanna.

Gary looked at Jonathan's face and poured his cousin a glass of wine. "Relax, will you? *We* survived the Ordeal."

"Barely." Jonathan drained his glass.

"Barely, perhaps, but we survived. She will, too. And remember this: we're taught that the magic of the Chamber can't be influenced by *anything*. When she passes the Ordeal, no one will be able to say she didn't earn her shield, whether she's a girl or not."

Alanna emerged from the bath, dried and dressed. She was a little pale, Gary noticed, but otherwise calm. "Are you prepared to be instructed?" he asked formally.

Alanna licked dry lips. This was where it began. "I am," she whispered.

"If you survive the Ordeal of Knighthood," Jonathan said, using the words required by the ritual, "you will be a Knight of the Realm. You will be sworn to protect those weaker than you, to obey your overlord, to live in a way that honors your kingdom and your gods."

"To wear the shield of a knight is an important thing," Gary went on. "It means you may not ignore a cry for help. It means that rich and poor, young and old, male and female may look to you for rescue, and you cannot deny them."

"You are bound to uphold the law," Jonathan said. "You may not look away from wrongdoing. You may not help anyone to break the law of the land, and you must prevent the breaking of the law at all times, in all cases."

"You are bound to your honor and your word," Gary reminded her. "Act in such a way that when you face the Dark God you need not be ashamed."

"You have learned the laws of Chivalry," Jonathan continued. "Keep them in your heart. Use them as your guides when things are their darkest. They will not fail you if you interpret them with humanity and kindness. A knight is gentle. A knight's first duty is to understand."

Alanna listened carefully. None of this was new, but tonight it had more meaning than it ever had before. Tonight she would hold vigil in the chapel outside the Chamber of the Ordeal—the first step toward proving herself finally worthy of a knight's shield. And tomorrow?

I'll think about tomorrow tomorrow, she told herself firmly.

Gary and Jon took her to the Chapel of the Ordeal, stopping only to remind her that she could not utter a sound between that point and the time when she stepped out of the Chamber the next day. Gary patted her on the shoulder, and Jonathan kissed her cheek. Then they were gone, and she was alone in the Chapel, looking at the heavy iron door leading to the Chamber. Four years ago she had knelt here beside Jonathan, watching his face and wondering what he was thinking. Now it was her turn, and she still had no idea of what his thoughts had been that night. Was his heart beating too fast, as hers did now? Had he been scared? This not being able to talk was hard. There was nothing a would-be knight could do but think.

After a while her thoughts drifted. Coram had arrived two nights ago. They had remained up for the better part of the night while he gave her his last report as steward of Trebond. Now young Armen had the dubious joy of that post, and Alanna's old friend was looking forward to being on the road with her. She was proud that her first teacher had been impressed by how far she had come in four years. Alanna refused his compliments, pointing out that if she had done well, it was because he had taught her well. The remainder of the night had been spent poring over maps, deciding where they would go in search of adventure. Alanna smiled a little sadly to herself.

Funny, she thought. *It used to be I couldn't wait to go. And now that the time to leave is here, I only want to stay. Why can't I be happy—or at least, why can't I make up my mind?*

Where was Thom? He had planned to be at the palace by Midwinter Festival, but so far there was no sign of him. Had he forgotten her in pursuit of some weird old spell? In some ways he reminded her of their father, who had spent much of his life in a scholarly dream.

She let her thoughts roam. Touching the ember-stone she remembered the dark night she had met the Great Goddess. Why had the Mother given her the stone? Was it a weapon, or a keepsake?

She thought of Jonathan. *Marrying him wouldn't be so bad, someday,* she realized. Yet that was impossible; he had to marry for the good of Tortall. And certainly she didn't want to marry *now;* she had too much to do!

Duke Roger. So many strange things had happened over the years that forced her to wonder what he was doing. And yet she had never pursued her suspicions very far—why not? Was she simply jealous of Jonathan's colorful relative and of the hold Roger had over people? Or did she have real cause to think he meant her prince ill? The Goddess had tried to warn her, in a very subtle way. Did the gods want Alanna to confront Roger?

And with what? she thought rebelliously. *I have no proof against him, and no way to obtain proof. I would lose everything—honor, reputation, friends, perhaps even my life—if I accused Roger without solid evidence in my hands. I hope the gods don't think I'm that reckless—or that stupid!*

Suddenly she blinked. Light was touching the high windows of the Chapel, and the dark-robed priests were filing into the room. One touched her shoulder, pointing to the heavy iron door. It was time for the Ordeal.

Alanna got up stiffly, wincing at the pain in her knees. Where had the night gone? Rubbing her shoulders and grimacing, she followed the silent priest to the front of the Chapel. Her attention fixed on the men unbarring the door of the Chamber, until that was all she saw. Her heart pounding furiously, her mouth dry, she did not realize that behind her the Chapel was filling with her friends.

Silently the door to the Chamber of the Ordeal swung open. Swallowing hard, Alanna braced her shoulders and walked inside. Swiftly the priests closed the door, leaving her in total darkness, just as she had so often dreamed.

She blinked, letting her eyes get used to the light inside the Chamber. Oddly enough, there *was* light, although there were no torches or windows. It was ghostly, but it was there. Hope flared up in her heart. Perhaps she would be all right.

She was in a small stone room. It was completely bare of furnishings or fixtures. There were no doors or windows, no way anything could enter, and Alanna was beginning to wonder if this were some kind of joke when the first blast of icy wind knocked her to her knees. Alanna hugged herself, her teeth chattering, her clothes no protection at all. *I wish I was dressed for this,* she thought, forcing down the panic that washed over her whenever she was too cold.

The harsh wind whipped through her, forcing her down again every time she tried to stand, numbing her hands and feet. Alanna tried to move about, slapping herself to get warm, but the wind pushed her flat against the floor, making it almost impossible to move. She fought it with all her strength, her lower lip gripped between her teeth. She even forgot her fear; the only important thing now was to stay alive.

Suddenly she heard voices. The wind stopped as abruptly as it began.

The voices rose, begging Alanna to help them, to rescue them from the Dark God. She recognized them: her father, Big Thor, boys who had died during the Sweating Sickness, men who were killed fighting Tusaine. Tears rolled down her cheeks; she wanted to help them, but there was just no way that she could. They belonged to the Dark God now. As much as she hated it, she was helpless.

The voices stopped.

Alanna stood, slowly, feeling herself tremble. What next?

Something in the corner behind her clicked. Alanna spun and quickly bit her fist to keep from screaming. She must not cry out! But how was she expected to stay silent when a spider the size of a horse advanced on her? She *hated* spiders!

Backing into a corner, she gritted her teeth together so hard they hurt. The spider came on, clicking hungrily. It brushed her with a long, hairy foreleg...

And then she was drowning, just as she nearly had drowned when she was five and again last winter, when someone salted the ice on the skating pond. Not for the first time she wondered if *she* had been meant to drown beneath that weakened ice. She could not forget that Alex had been there once again, and Alex had challenged her to skate. *Odd thoughts to have when you're drowning, I suppose,* she mused as she fought her way up. Her strength was running out, and even the discovery that she couldn't reach the surface resulted in nothing more than exhausted dismay.

No, she thought. *I won't cry out. I'll die if I have to, but I won't cry out.*

The ocean was gone. Alanna knelt on the Chamber floor, taking huge breaths of air as silently as she could and wondered what would happen next. Her skin and clothes were completely dry.

Nothing happened. Alanna waited, not quite cringing, afraid that whatever this demon-place threw at her would be worse than anything that had gone before. Finally she began to pace, rubbing her arms. She was still very cold. Cold, being helpless against death, spiders, drowning; the Chamber made her live vividly with everything she most feared. Was that what the Ordeal was about, making would-be knights face their fears?

She sneezed and looked up. The air was humming with power, and a pale blotch was spreading against one stone wall. It was filled with colors and shapes, but they did not resolve into the picture they seemed to form. Alanna narrowed her eyes to see if they would come into focus, but the picture remained hazy. Something told her it was important—even vital—for her to see that vision clearly, no matter what the cost. She strained against the haze, reaching out toward the wall. Her hands hit something solid, almost clothlike, keeping her from the vision. Alanna gritted her teeth and gripped the invisible stuff in her hands, feeling fine threads cut into her palms as she tried to tear a hole through which she could see. Sweat poured down her cheeks, and she forgot how cold she was as her fingers found some invisible opening. She tugged hard, the sinews in her arms cramping with the effort.

A barrier in front of her—magical or real, she had no way of knowing—gave way, and she fell forward onto her knees. The picture on the wall was clear, too clear.

A triumphant, smiling Roger stood beside Jonathan's bed. Alanna's Prince lay on it, his hands crossed on his chest, and a crown on his head. Jon was whiter than marble, the white of death. Laughing soundlessly, Roger took the crown from Jonathan's head and put it on his own.

Alanna threw herself at the picture, opening her mouth to scream. Only at the last moment did she remember to remain silent; she bit her lip to keep her mouth closed. Her mind continued to scream *No!* as she beat her fists raw on the invisible wall that kept her away from Duke Roger. At last she dropped to the floor, tears streaming down her cheeks.

No! she thought, clenching her bruised and bloody hands. *It won't happen! I won't let it happen! I will never let Jonathan die!*

Slowly the Chamber door opened. She stumbled out, her hands torn and bloody, her mouth a thin, tight line. Jon and Myles hurried forward to help her out of the Chapel, Faithful and Coram following. The Prince put healing salve on her hands and bandaged them before the men put her to bed.

Alanna looked at him, her eyelids already heavy. "It won't happen, Jon. I promise it won't."

Jonathan wiped the sweat-soaked hair away from her forehead. "I know it won't," he whispered. "Now, sleep. It's over."

"It's *not* over," she wanted to say, but she was too tired. Her eyes shut, and she slept soundly without dreams. She had not spoken—or screamed—at all.

∾

The Ceremony of Knighthood at sunset was brief. The *real* ceremony, the Ordeal, was over, and this was just a formality. Alanna knelt before the King and gave her oath of fealty, swearing to defend the crown and Tortall all of her life. In turn, the King touched his sword to Alanna's shoulders and head, saying gently, "I dub thee Sir Alan, Knight of the Realm of Tortall. Serve honorably and well."

Alanna stood. It was strange. She didn't feel any

different, except tired and shaken, but now she was a knight.

A slender, red-bearded man stepped out of the crowd, beckoning Coram forward. Thom grinned at his startled twin. "Your Majesties," he said politely, bowing to the King and Queen, "I am Thom, Lord of Trebond, and a Master of the Mithran Light. I beg leave, by right of my relationship to Sir Alan, to present him with his shield." He gestured toward the large, leather-covered object Coram bore.

The King inclined his head, refusing to stare at the very young Master as his Court was doing. "You have the right, Lord Thom."

Thom removed the shield cover, revealing a black tower on a red field: the Trebond arms. Taking it from Coram, Alanna settled it on her left arm. It was light and strong, and she could feel the protecting spells on it. She bowed to her brother and to the King and Queen, then glanced around, startled by the sound of cheers. They were cheering her! She shook her head, blushing. They had cheered when Jonathan was knighted, of course, but this was something else. He was the heir, and an heir who was a knight was far more powerful than an heir who wasn't. But she found a place in their hearts, and they cheered her because they loved her.

Thom went with her to her room to put the shield away. He greeted Faithful solemnly as Alanna placed the shield on her bed in order to look it over.

"I thought you weren't going to be here after all," she observed, touching the shield with a bandaged hand. "This is beautiful."

"I was held up because I wanted to make it secretly. Watch this." Smiling slightly, he passed his hand over the shield's face. Alanna stared as the black tower faded, leaving instead a great gold cat on its hind legs.

"What is it?" she asked as the cat faded and the tower reappeared. Thom helped her put the cover on the shield and hang it in her dressing room with her other arms.

"It's a lioness rampant, of course. For when you reveal what you really are. Let's go to dinner; I'm starved."

Alanna led the way to the banquet hall, thinking: *A lioness rampant. I like it.*

ten

To Duel the Sorcerer

*T*he second feast of the Midwinter Festival had begun, with nearly every noble of Roald's Court present. Thom excused himself to Alanna with a wink and went to sit with Duke Roger, who showed no sign of bad feeling toward a younger, and maybe stronger, sorcerer. Alanna watched them talk for a few moments before turning her attention to other people there. The Queen had made a rare appearance. It was the first time Alanna had seen Jonathan's mother in public since her illness more than a year before. Lianne seemed to be holding her own for a while, but slowly she turned very pale. From her seat among the other knights, Alanna could see beads of sweat on Lianne's face, and the Queen's fingers trembled as she tried to raise her wine glass. When she began to cough, Duke Baird rushed to her, his face tense and worried.

Remembering her vision in the Chamber of the Ordeal, Alanna grabbed the ember-stone at her throat. She bit her lower lip; as she had feared, Queen Lianne was glowing a faint but steady orange.

Suddenly Alanna was filled with the need to act, and to act *now*. If Roger had placed magic of any kind on the Queen, there would have to be physical evidence of some kind, somewhere, Even the most powerful sorcerer had to have a real object as the focus of his thoughts.

Alanna waited until the feast was in full swing before excusing herself, promising her friends she would only be gone a few moments. *Now* was the time, while Roger's attention was fully occupied with Thom and the questions her brother represented. The King would not rise for another hour at least. Alanna planned to use that hour.

Feeling as if she had gained a new life and a sharper way of looking at things in the Chamber of the Ordeal, she hurried back to her chamber. Most of her belongings were packed, since she would be moving in the morning to her own rooms. Faithful, exiled from the feast, was waiting for her.

You are taking a risk, the cat said as Alanna searched her trunk for the new lock-picks George had given her. *If he catches you, you will be very dead.*

"Then he mustn't catch me. Agreed?" Alanna shoved the leather envelope holding the picks into her tunic. "Come on. You stand guard."

Faithful trotted along as she took the back halls that led to Roger's rooms. *There must be insanity in my family, too.*

Alanna grinned but did not answer.

Roger's suite of rooms was located very conveniently for Alanna's purposes. A small flight of stairs twisted up and away from the hall, ending with Roger's outer door. While Faithful stood guard at the foot of the steps, Alanna set to work, hidden from view by the turn in the wall.

Carefully she inserted the first pick into the lock. It flared and melted. Alanna quickly dropped it, swearing silently at her own stupidity. Of course Roger would put guarding-spells on his doors. She eyed the lock resentfully, deciding what to do next. It would take too long to try a spell that would lift the guards, and she was in a hurry. There *was* another way...

Placing her bandaged hands on the lock. Alanna drew a deep breath. Fiercely she *shoved* her magic into the lock, literally exploding Roger's spell. After her eyes cleared from the blinding flash that resulted, Alanna warily tried another lockpick. It took the work of only a second before she heard the tumblers fall into place. The door swung open, and she whistled softly for Faithful. The cat ran swiftly inside; Alanna closed the door behind them.

There was no point in searching the main rooms. What she was looking for would not be here. People came and went in these rooms every day; Roger wouldn't leave anything important there. In the rear of the suite, however, was a closed door that led to Roger's workroom. It too was locked.

Using her ember-stone as a guide, Alanna could see the orange fire gleaming around the door. She had expected that. As with the front door, she had no time to figure out which spell would lift the guards, even if she knew the right spell, which she doubted. The guards on *this* door would be far more powerful than those on the main door.

Steeling herself, Alanna placed her hands against the door and thrust her magic out. This time she fainted.

Faithful brought her around by licking her nose with his rough tongue. *Sleep later,* he said.

She sneered elegantly at her pet and opened the sorcerer's door.

All around the room were counters littered with instruments, herbs and books. Alanna glanced at the books; she knew some of them and she had heard of others. Most were books on magic. Some she could not read because they were written in a completely alien script. She noticed seeing-crystals of varying sizes and colors: clear, pink and black. One was blood red, and she refused to touch it. The large charcoal-burning dishes stood in the center of the room for heat. Instead of torches, Roger used lamps that burned with a bright, unflickering light.

"Do I hear splashing?" she asked Faithful softly. she looked around carefully, at last spotting a fountain at the back of the room. Water poured from a spout in the wall, dancing over rocks covered with flowering moss before falling into a deep basin.

Curious at the fountain's existence, Alanna went to look at it more closely.

Two things caught her interest: a silvery-white veil that seemed to hold several objects, and a doll, immersed in the fountain's basin directly under the waterspout. For a moment Alanna wanted to touch neither bundle nor doll, but her newfound resolution forced her to pick up both. She carried them over to one of the counters, drawing a lamp close to examine her finds.

The doll was a water-worn wax image of the Queen, perfect from the real black hairs on its head to the duplicate of the Queen's favorite gown. The doll had obviously been in the water for a long time: the features of its face were barely recognizable, and the color had washed from its dress. Alanna knew this spell: the sorcerer made an image of his victim and placed it in running water. Depending on the sorcerer's materials and power, and the strength of the water, the one represented by the doll wasted away quickly or slowly, fading into death. Duke Roger had used the finest wax money could buy, and Alanna suspected he had taken the doll out of the fountain from time to time, to make the Queen's illness and eventual death seem more natural.

Her hands trembling, Alanna put the doll aside and looked at the bundle she had also found. Lifting it less carefully this time, she saw the tear in the side too late. Another tiny doll fell out of the bundle, striking the table. Alanna yelled, her side suddenly one massive hurt. Biting her fist to keep from making any more noise, she picked the image up. It was one of her, of course. She examined the bundle closely. The tear was long and thin, nearly invisible against the fine-woven silk. Her hands throbbed, and she remembered how they had felt the morning of her Ordeal, as if she was trying to tear a hole in tightly woven cloth. Drawing her dagger, she cut the string that held the bundle closed and carefully opened it up on the table's surface. Figures that bore eerie resemblances to the King, Duke Gareth, Myles, the Lord Provost, and even Jonathan lay revealed before her eyes.

"Of course," she told Faithful softly. "Now I understand. He wanted none of us to see what he was up to, so he put our images inside this veil. We couldn't see; and as long as men like Duke Gareth or Myles or the Provost didn't see anything wrong, no one else felt they could say anything."

What are you going to do now? Faithful inquired, twitching his tail. *You've broken all those silly rules of Chivalry to get yourself this far. What next?*

Alanna smiled grimly at the images, carefully piling them on top of the veil. "Roger can't be allowed to go on this way," she replied. "When he comes back tonight, he'll know the images are gone; he may even know I took them. So, if my friends and I are to survive his finding out, I'd bet-

ter do something about Duke Roger of Conté right
now."

∽

She returned to the banquet hall, the veil and its
contents in her hands. Stopping for a moment to
talk to Myles and Jonathan, she asked them to join
her before the King's table. Thom was exchanging
stories with Raoul and Gary, but when he caught
his sister's eye, he excused himself and came to
stand next to her. Steeling herself, Alanna walked
up to the long table in front of the two thrones,
bowing low to the King and Queen. Only when she
felt Myles, Thom and Jonathan at her back, did she
begin to speak.

Great Mother, help me with this, she pleaded
silently when Roald acknowledged her. *I don't know
if this is how you wanted me to do this, but it's the
only way I know.*

"Majesty," she said clearly, making sure everyone could hear her voice, "I have done a dishonorable thing." The great hall was suddenly quiet.
Alanna drew a deep breath and went on. "I broke
into a man's chambers tonight. I knew this was dishonorable, and I did it anyway. What *I* did was
wrong. What I thought to find—what I *did* find—
was far worse."

She placed the veil and the images inside it on
the table before the King. Lianne cried out in horror, shrinking away from the little dolls made to

represent her, her husband, her son and her brother. The King and Duke Gareth were pale; the Provost, peering around his neighbor's shoulder, turned red with fury. Thom reached out curiously for a moment before remembering it would not be a good idea to handle those images. There was no reading the emotions either Jonathan or Myles was feeling—perhaps it was just as well.

Alanna looked at Duke Roger. The sorcerer could see what she had put before his uncle; he was gripping the arms of his chair with white-knuckled hands.

"Shall I tell them where I found these, Your Grace?" Alanna challenged loudly, looking the Duke of Conté in the eyes. "Shall I tell them about the little fountain in your private workroom where the Queen's image lay under running water, wasting away little by little? Shall I—"

"Liar!" Roger snarled. "Majesty, *Sir* Alan has long been jealous of my influence with you and my cousin Jonathan. He now seeks to dishonor me in your eyes by showing you these dolls *he* created and accusing me of casting such spells!"

"For what reason?" Alanna asked King Roald. "Why would I wish the Queen harm? She is the mother of my Prince and my friend. She has been kind to me. I do not gain by harming her, just as I do not gain from veiling the sight of those who could stop me from stealing a throne that isn't mine!"

"Liar!" Roger cried, standing to point an accusing finger at her. "Do you deny that you have the skill to place such a spell? Do you deny you have the knowledge, when I taught image-magic to you myself? You planned to kill Their Majesties, so that when Jonathan became King, *you* would be the most powerful knight in the realm."

"That is very interesting." Myles looked at Roger, his gentle eyes hard. "Carry that thinking a step further and suppose the death of Prince Jonathan. Who would gain? I submit, Roger, that *you* would gain as the next King of Tortall."

"It's a plot against me!" Roger cried, looking around him. "Myles tries to turn you all against me while this young man gives false evidence!" He stopped, waiting for the King to say something. The only sound in the banquet hall was the Queen weeping softly into Duke Gareth's shoulder. Roger looked for a friendly face and found none. His mouth tightened. "I demand my rights. I demand trial by combat, myself against my accuser." He pointed to Alanna. "If I lie, Sir Alan will win by the will of the gods. But I say *I* will win, because I am innocent!"

The silence grew as everyone waited for King Roald's decision. The King picked up the image of himself, turning it over in his fingers. "You may have the combat," he said.

"As the accused, I may choose the time," Roger said quickly. "Let it be now, before Sir Alan's lies spread and poison people's minds against me."

Alanna felt chilly and very old. She should have known that Roger would want to fight now, while she was still weary and sore from the Ordeal. She looked at her bandaged hands.

"This time or any other is of no matter to me," she said, her voice bored. "I believe Duke Roger to be plotting against the lives of my Prince and my friends. The sooner this is resolved, the sooner they will be safe."

"In one hour," ruled the King. "We meet in the Great Throne Room."

〜

*A*lanna slipped away and went to her room to change while Faithful watched. Since the rules of trial by combat forbade the wearing of armor, she changed into a soft shirt, breeches and stockings; she wanted as much freedom of movement as possible. Removing her bandages, she carefully rubbed balm into her sore hands, thinking, *Lucky they aren't stiff.* After lightly rebandaging her hands, she tied back her hair.

Sitting down to clean Lightning, she told Faithful, "I guess I don't feel so bad about not having spotted what he was up to. But why tonight? That hole in the veil didn't just *happen* to be there. Come in!" she called in answer to the knock on her door.

Jonathan, Myles, Coram and Thom entered the

room. Myles looked at her wearily. "I suppose you had your reasons for acting as you did. I'd like to know what they were."

Alanna shook her head. "It's as if I just broke free of the spell he had us all under. A lot of things just began to add up: why the fog came up that night I was taken *after* he visited me, why the big Tusaine attack was chiefly aimed at Jonathan's forces, why the Queen never got better. Thom, you must've thought I was crazy, never following up on the warnings you and George gave me."

Thom shrugged. "I always figured you had your reasons." Jonathan, Myles and Coram looked at him, and the young Master added, "I've been watched by Duke Roger's men for several years, ever since you, Highness, and Alan took the Black City. And George has waylaid Roger's men following Alan any number of times."

Coram took over the cleaning of Lightning while Alanna began to stretch. Her body was stiff from the Ordeal, and she had seen Roger enough in the fencing courts to know he would not be easy to beat even if she were feeling her best. That he was a sorcerer and not a trained knight was balanced by the fact that, for all she knew, he was sticking pins into a new image of her at that very moment.

Jonathan looked down at Alanna, who was touching her toes. "But you had suspicions," he pointed out. "Even if they were vague ones, why didn't you talk to me?"

"I *did* say something, at the Black City," she told him frankly. "You said it was nonsense. So I wanted to have real proof before I mentioned it again. And every time I made up my mind to *do* something about it, I—I lost interest. I know why now— because he had me in the wraps with you and Myles and the others—but I still feel ashamed that it happened. Don't you?"

Before Jonathan could say that he did understand, someone else knocked on Alanna's door. Coram opened it and admitted a heavily cloaked George.

Jonathan and Myles were clearly astonished by the tall Rogue's presence. "Stefan has messenger-birds," Alanna told them. She gave the thief a tiny smile before beginning to stretch again. "I'm glad you came."

George reached down to ruffle her hair with a gentle hand. "Do nothing foolish," he warned her.

"I think Alan's used up his foolishness for the day," Thom said acidly.

Alanna looked up, impatient. "The masquerade is over. Myles, all these men know, you should, too. I'm a girl."

"But I *do* know," Myles said quietly. "Thank you for telling me at last, but I have known for years."

Timon rapped on the door and opened it. "I've been sent to bring you to the Great Throne Room," he said unhappily. "Squire—Sir Alan, is it true? About His Grace?"

Alanna tugged on her boots. Her mouth was suddenly very dry. "Yes. It's true."

"Alan and I will be with you in a moment," Jonathan told the others. They took the hint and followed Timon out into the hall, closing the door behind them. Alanna looked at Jonathan and went into his arms, hugging him tightly.

"I'm sorry," she whispered, fighting back tears. "I know you love him; but I couldn't let it go on. He was killing your mother."

Jonathan held her close. "I love you more." His voice was breaking. "Don't let him kill you."

Alanna shook her head. "I don't plan to. Believe me, I don't."

They joined the other men in the hall. No one spoke as they headed for the Great Throne Room. Their only comments were in the tight holds Jonathan and George took on each of her shoulders, and the worried looks Coram, Myles and Thom wore. Matters now were beyond words.

Alanna herself could think only that finally it had come to a head, this weird contest of wills between her and the Duke of Conté. The issue would be decided once and for all. She couldn't be unhappy about that. *It'll be over and settled,* she thought as they strode into the Great Throne Room.

Roger already stood before the two thrones, naked sword in hand. Alanna hugged each of her friends one last time before stepping up beside

Roger, Lightning unsheathed and ready for battle. Her heart pounded in her throat as the herald read the challenge. She could barely hear him; her attention was on the King and Queen, on Jon, standing beside his father now, and on Duke Gareth, standing beside his sister, the Queen. She felt a grim kind of triumph, thinking, *Even if he kills me, I've won. I've planted the seed of doubt here; he'll never be trusted again.*

It was good to know she had accomplished something, even if Roger killed her. And it was good to know her friends were there, wanting her to win.

"Let the combat begin," Roald said quietly.

Alanna and Roger brought their swords up instantly. They circled, watching each other carefully. Roger feinted at Alanna several times, never intending to strike, instead trying to draw Alanna into an attack. Alanna smiled slightly. Roger was older than she was and more experienced in the ways of the world, but she could outwait him.

She was right. Roger attacked in earnest, thinking she was being overconfident. Alanna blocked his swing and dodged to the side, wincing as Lightning jarred against her sore hands. She would have to be careful; her stiffness and the pain in her hands might get her killed if she wasn't.

Roger pursued the attack, trying to use up her energy. Alanna tried to dodge more and block less in order to spare herself, but the sorcerer was too quick. Pain wormed its way up her right arm and into her shoulder. The scrapes on her sword hand were bleeding through the bandages, and weariness put her timing off.

Suddenly she blinked. Had Roger switched his sword to his left hand, or was he carrying two swords? He couldn't *possibly* have two blades! She shook her head, trying to clear her eyes. Dimly she could hear Thom yelling, "Foul! He's using an illusion!" But she knew no one would try to stop the fight now, for fear of getting her killed.

Only a lucky step saved her life as the Duke lunged at her. Thom was right: the Duke had placed an illusion-spell on himself so that Alanna couldn't tell which of his hands gripped the *real* sword and which held only the ghost of one. Alanna pulled the ember-stone from beneath her shirt with her free hand, thanking the Goddess for it. The illusion-sword now glowed orange in her eyes. She blocked Roger's real sword and thrust back, coming body-to-body with the Duke. This was a mistake; the larger, stronger man used his strength to force her slowly to her knees.

Alanna gasped and broke, dropping to the floor and rolling away. Roger struck, cutting her shoulder open as Alanna came to her feet. She dodged back, biting her lip angrily; he had changed his sword to his left hand! She thanked the Goddess the cut was not bad and gripped the ember-stone again.

The Duke switched hands several times, but

she was able to follow the changing of real and imaginary swords with the help of the stone. They were coming to a time in the battle she was too familiar with: the time when lesser swordsmen began to gasp for air and to make mistakes, the time when she had to reach deep inside herself for strength she rarely needed to draw upon. Forced to admire Roger's technique as she grimly blocked and thrust, lunged and dodged, she couldn't help but think that it was too bad such an awful man was such a fine swordsman.

Seizing that brief moment when Roger switched swords, Alanna lunged in, slashing the Duke's right arm. Roger yelled in fury as Lightning nipped through muscle. Making an impossibly quick recovery, the Duke lunged back and struck. Alanna stumbled, and the tip of Duke Roger's sword sliced down her chest from collarbone to waist.

The special corset she often wore in place of bandaging gave way, its laces cut through. It slid and buckled under her shirt, edges of lace-strings and (to Alanna's great embarrassment) the curves of her breasts showing through.

Roger dropped his blade and stood back, his eyes wide with shock.

"Halt!" the King roared, coming to his feet. The crowded room was buzzing as he stared at Alanna. *"What is going on here?"*

"You'd better do something about that thing,"

Thom advised, stepping forward. "I'll explain."

All eyes were fixed on the Master in silver-edged black as Alanna ducked behind a hanging curtain, suddenly glad her lie was over with. She slid the ruined corset out from under her slashed shirt as Thom said, "You'll have to excuse my sister, Majesties." Shaking her head over her brother's nerve, she overlapped the ends of the shirt and tucked them firmly into her breeches.

"You see, she wanted to be a knight," Thom was explaining. "I wanted to be a sorcerer. We traded places. I think I may have had the better part of the bargain; I didn't have to lie to people I liked and respected all these years. Here. I brought our birth papers. Her name is Alanna. We're twins."

"Who knew of this?" The King's voice was low and dangerous as Alanna stepped out from behind the curtain. "*Who knew?*"

"I knew." Jonathan's voice was strong and clear. "I've known since the Black City."

"I knew," Coram admitted in a shamefaced rumble.

Gary stepped forward. "I knew."

"And I knew," Myles added. "I guessed when Alan—Alanna—cured Jonathan of the Sweating Sickness, Majesty."

The King looked at Alanna. "What have you to say for yourself?"

Alanna met his eyes squarely. "I hated lying to you," she admitted. "I wanted to tell; but I couldn't.

Would you have let me win my shield if I had told the truth?" The King's silence was answer enough. "I've tried to be honest about everything else. And I can't regret what I did."

Roger's snarl of fury surprised them all. "You *demon!*" he screamed. "You lying, cheating—"

Without warning he lunged at her, his sword raised. Alanna blocked him and fought for her life. Roger attacked like a whirlwind, not giving her a chance to catch her breath.

Suddenly Alanna's long-hidden anger toward Roger flared into life. He was her enemy; he had tried to kill the people she loved. And *he* was acting like the wronged one!

She set her jaw grimly. She had come here to bring Duke Roger of Conté to justice, and by the Mother, that was what she was going to do.

She brought Lightning up and around in a wide butterfly-sweep that slicked off a lock of Roger's hair. Switching her sword to her left hand, she attacked in earnest at last, bringing her blade down and around in a mirror image of the first butterfly-sweep, slicing Roger's belt. She came around with a back-handed slash that ripped open the Duke's tunic. Desperate, Roger blocked and fell back as she came on, a grim vision of death.

Suddenly a large orange cloud formed around the Duke. The watching nobles gasped and moved away as the cloud expanded, reaching for Alanna and for Jonathan and for King Roald beside

Jonathan. Alanna saw the danger to the two men and forgot her own.

"The Goddess!" she yelled, leaping forward. Lightning struck the cloud, slicing it open to find Roger at its heart. The orange mass flared, blinding everyone watching. Alanna felt Lightning quiver. Roger screamed; and she struck again, harder. The sword cut even deeper this time as Alanna opened her eyes, blinking to clear her vision.

Roger stood, trying to pull her sword out of his body. A deep cut in his shoulder was bleeding fiercely. The Duke stared wonderingly at Alanna as he slowly fell to the floor. Alanna jerked Lightning free of him, swaying over Roger's body, shaking with rage, fear and exhaustion.

She looked up. Everyone in the chamber—even Jonathan, even Thom—stared at her with some kind of horror. For a minute she was afraid of herself.

She had killed the King's nephew. She had killed her greatest enemy, the most powerful sorcerer in the Eastern Lands.

Epilogue

"*A*re you sure you won't change your mind?" Jonathan asked, taking her hand. The winter breeze whipped color into his cheeks, making his eyes seem bluer than ever. "I really feel I don't know 'Sir Alanna' at all."

Alanna smiled and shook her head. "I need to be alone; well, not exactly *alone*," she admitted, grinning at the bundled-up Coram. "I need to get away from Court for a while and just think."

"If you're still feeling bad about Roger, you shouldn't," Gary said tartly. "You did what had to be done."

"I know. But I've been planning this journey for a long time, and now I have more reason than ever to take it. I'll sort out Roger and being a lady knight and what I want to do with my life, and then I'll come back." She looked around, making sure that her saddlebags, as well as those on the pack mule, were secure. She glanced up at her worried escort—Jonathan, Gary, Raoul and George—and smiled at them. "Truly I will. I couldn't stay away long."

Gary tapped the miserable-looking Raoul on the shoulder. "Say goodbye, Raoul," he said, glancing meaningfully at Jon.

Raoul took one of Alanna's hands in a grip that hurt. "I'm like Jonathan; I just don't feel I know 'Sir Alanna,'" he complained. "Look out for her, Coram."

"I will that." The burly manservant nodded.

Alanna leaned over and kissed Raoul on the cheek. "This 'Sir Alanna' you keep talking about is just Alan with the truth being told," she told him. "I haven't changed. Stay out of trouble, Raoul."

Gary was next, giving her a brief but strong hug. "If you stay away too long, we'll come looking for you," he threatened. "Safe, journey, Alanna." He drew Raoul off a little way, leaving Alanna to talk with Jonathan and George in peace.

"Remember the thieves' sign I taught you," George warned. "And if trouble threatens, use it!"

Alanna hugged him, blinking back stinging tears. "I'm going to miss you, old friend," she whispered.

George's eyes were overbright as he smiled at her. "So much more reason for you to return to me, after you've thought through all that needs thinkin'. Go with my love, Alanna." Clucking to his mare, he caught up with Gary and Raoul.

Jonathan tried to smile in his turn. "And so it's just you and me again, Lady Knight. Well, you and me and Faithful," he acknowledged the cat, who sat blinking in his cup on Moonlight's saddle. Suddenly he reached over and hugged her tightly, holding her for long moments. He kissed her fiercely before letting her go. "You're riding south?"

Alanna nodded. "I want to spend the rest of this winter being *warm*," she told him. "I'll write; you know I will."

He lifted her face, looking into her violet eyes. "When you come home, all this will have blown over," he said. "And no one will be happier to see you than I." He looked over at Coram, who was waiting by the City Gates. "Take care of her, Coram Smythesson!"

Alanna's old friend looked surprised. "And here I thought the best part of ridin' with a knight was that *she* would be lookin' after *me*."

Alanna exchanged one last look with her Prince before riding out the gate. Before her stretched the Great Road South, its broad expanse clear of snow and ice. It was almost warm for the first day of New Year; she was dressed comfortably; she had a good horse and Faithful with her and Coram at her side.

Roger's death was bad, she thought, *but life could be much, much worse. Perhaps I'll live and be happy after all.*

She let out a whoop of sheer exuberance and kicked Moonlight into a gallop. "C'mon, Coram!" she cried, galloping past him. "Let's go find an adventure!"

*T*AMORA PIERCE was born in western Pennsylvania in 1954, has lived in various states across America, and currently resides in Manhattan. A graduate of the University of Pennsylvania, she studied social work, film, and psychology. She has been a martial arts movie reviewer, housemother in a group home, a literary agent's assistant, head writer for a radio production company, and an investment banking secretary. She is married to writer/film-maker Tim Liebe. They are owned by two cats (the Lioness, better known as Scrap, and Vinnie) and by Zorak, an attitudinal parakeet.

Ms. Pierce began writing stories when she was eleven. Her published books include the Song of the Lioness quartet (*Alanna: The First Adventure, In the Hand of the Goddess, The Woman Who Rides Like a Man,* and *Lioness Rampant*) and the Immortals quartet (*Wild Magic, Wolf-Speaker, Emperor Mage,* and *The Realms of the Gods*), which have also been translated into German and Danish. Ms. Pierce has already started working on her next series.

Turn the page for a preview of
Alanna's continuing adventures in

The Woman Who Rides Like a Man

Song of the Lioness
Book Three

—now a Random House Fantasy paperback

𝒜lanna of Trebond, the sole woman knight in the realm of Tortall, splashed happily in the waters of an oasis, enjoying her first bath in three days. *Hard to believe that it's winter in the North,* she reflected. In the Southern Desert the temperatures were just right, although she objected to so much sand.

"Best hurry up," Coram told her. Her burly man-at-arms stood guard on the other side of the bushes that concealed the pool. "If this is a Bazhir waterin' place, we don't want to wait and find out if they swear for the King or against him."

Alanna stepped out of the water, grabbing her clothes. She had no urge to meet any Bazhir tribesmen, particularly not renegades. She and Coram were bound for Tyra in the south, and coming to battle with the warlike desert men would cut their journey very short.

Drying off, the young knight pulled on a boy's blue shirt and breeches. Although her femininity was not the secret it had been when she trained in the royal palace, Alanna still preferred the freedom of men's clothing. It was odd to remember that the last time she bathed in an oasis, she had been a page and Prince Jonathan had just found out she was girl. Those days—the days in which she bound her chest flat and never went swimming—were gone. She didn't miss them.

Faithful, her pet cat, was yowling a warning. "Alanna!" Coram yelled, seconding the cat. "We've got trouble!"

Grabbing her sword, Alanna raced for Coram and the horses. An approaching cloud of dust indicated tribesmen or robbers, and she grimaced as she threw herself into Moonlight's saddle. She trotted forward to meet Faithful, a small black streak racing toward her across the sand. The cat leaped, landing squarely in front of his mistress before climbing into the leather cup that was his position on her saddle. Alanna's gentle mare held steady, used to the cat's abrupt comings and goings.

"Let's try to reach the road!" Alanna told Coram.

They rode hard, Alanna crouched low over Moonlight's pale mane. She looked back to see Coram shaking his head. "It's no good," he was bellowing. "They've spotted us! Ride on—I'll hold 'em!"

Alanna wheeled and stopped, Lightning glittering in her hand. "What sort of friend d'you think I am? We'll wait for them here."

Coram swore. "If ye were my daughter, I'd tan yer hide! Go!"

Alanna shook her head stubbornly. She could see their pursuers now: they were hillmen, the worst of the desert raiders. Reaching behind her, she unbuckled her shield from its straps, slipping it over her left arm. Coram was following suit.

"Stubborn lass," he grumbled. "I'd druther tangle with ten Bazhir tribes than any hillmen."

Alanna nodded. The Bazhir were deadly fighters, but they had a strict code of honor. Hillmen lived for killing and loot.

Renewing her grip on Lightning's hilt, she settled her shield more firmly on her arm. The hillmen closed rapidly, fanning out in a half circle that would close around Alanna and her companion. Grimly the knight clenched her jaw and ordered, "Take them in a charge."

"*What?*" yelped Coram.

Alanna charged directly at the hillmen. Coram gulped and followed her, letting out a war cry.

Moonlight reared as they reached the first raiders, striking out with hooves: she had been trained for battle years ago. Alanna slashed about her with Lightning, ignoring her enemies' yells of fury.

A one-eyed villain closed in, grabbing her sword arm. With an angry yowl Faithful leaped from his cup with his claws unsheathed. The one-eyed hillman screamed and released Alanna, trying to pull the hissing cat away from his face.

"Lass! Beware!" Coram bellowed, trying to fend off three at once. He yelled in pain as one of them opened a deep gash on his sword arm. He swore and attacked again, dropping his shield and switching his sword to his good left hand.

Warned by her companion, Alanna whirled to face a giant hillman, a grinning mountain with red hair and long braided mustaches. He guided his shaggy pony with his knees, leaving his hands free to grip the hilt of a sword with an odd crystal blade. Alanna eyed its razor-sharp length and gulped, ducking beneath the redheaded man's first swing. He reversed it, and she blocked it with her shield just in time, yelping at the pain of impact. She struck back with Lightning, only to miss as her attacker darted away.

She refused to follow and fight on his terms. Instead she brought her lioness shield up and waited.

The giant returned, circling her carefully. His pony lunged forward, and Moonlight reared, warning it back with her flailing hooves. Alanna caught another blow from the crystal blade on her shield, feeling the shock through her entire body.

I hope my brother put plenty of magic on this shield, she thought grimly. Otherwise it won't last through its first battle!

She turned Moonlight as the giant circled her on his nimble pony. With a kick of her heels she urged the gold mare forward, slashing at her opponent. She was a knight of Tortall, and not be toyed with!

She used every chance to break through his guard. He blocked her time after time, grinning infuriatingly.

Alanna drew back, breathing hard and fighting to keep her control. Now the giant returned the attack, and she blinked sweat from her eyes: she could not afford to make a mistake now! His tactics were different from those of the mounted knights she had fought before; she didn't know what to expect.

Suddenly the midday sun was directly in her eyes—he had maneuvered her just for this. Only at the last second did she glimpse his sword descending on her. She brought Lightning up hard, slamming her blade hilt-to-hilt with the giant's sword. There was a ring of clashing metal, and the downward sweep of the crystal edge was stopped.

Then Lightning broke, sheared off near the hilt.

Moonlight darted away, taking Alanna out of the hillman's range. Her mistress stared at the hilt she still gripped. Lightning had been her sword ever since she had been considered fit to carry one. How could she fight without it in her hand?

Coming out of her daze, Alanna fumbled for her axe. She was trembling with rage: it took all her self-control to keep from losing her temper completely and making a fatal mistake. Axe in hand, she charged the hillman with a yell. She didn't hear the warning cries of the other hillmen, or Coram's gleeful whoop; she heard only the wheezing of the giant's pony and her own choked breath. She swung, swearing as the hillman ducked and pulled out of her range. She was closing with him again when he yelled, seeing something behind her. To her fury, he whirled his pony and fled, calling to the few men he had left. Alanna spurred after him.

"Come back, coward!" she cried.

The giant turned to laugh and shake his sword at her. His voice was choked off as a black arrow sprouted in his chest. More arrows struck down the hillmen; only two escaped. They rode for all they were worth, pursued by five white-robed tribesmen.

A Bazhir, his white burnoose tied with a scarlet cord, rode toward Alanna as she dismounted. She was staring at the body of the hillman who had wielded the crystal sword. The blade lay beside him, gleaming against the sand. It glimmered and suddenly flashed, blinding her for a short moment. Alanna stared: against the yellow-orange fire that filled her sight was a picture.

A dark finger—or was it a pole?—pointed at a crystal-blue sky. Before it stood a man wearing tattered gray; his eyes were mad. She could smell wood smoke.

Her eyes cleared, and the vision was gone.

Reaching under her shirt, Alanna drew forth the token given to her by the Great Mother Goddess three years before. It had once been a coal in her campfire; now it was covered in clear stone, its fires still flickering under its surface. Alanna knew that if she held it when magic was present, she could see power as a glowing force in the air. She saw magic now as orange light flickered around the sword, and she scowled. Recently she had dealt with magic of this particular shade, and the memory was not pleasant.

The Bazhir who had followed her kicked sand over the sword. "It is evil," he said, his quiet voice slightly raspy. "Let the desert have it."

Distracted from the magic, Alanna discovered she was crying. It was as if she had lost a companion, not a weapon.

A glint of metal caught her eye and she stopped to pick up Lightning's sheared-off blade. Sliding the length of metal into its sheath, she strapped the now-useless hilt in place. Unless she tried to draw the blade, no one would know it was not whole.

Mounting her horse, she settled Faithful before her as Coram brought his gelding to her side. "I'm sorry, lass," he told her quietly, putting a hand on her arm. "I know what the sword meant to ye. But ye can't be thinking of that now. These men may be friends or may not be; who knows why they saved

our skins. Ye'd best be puttin' yer mind to talk with
'em."

Alanna nodded, trying to collect her thoughts.
Their rescuers formed a loose circle around her and
Coram as the man who had covered the crystal
sword with sand joined them, guiding a large chestnut stallion with ease. The others gave way to him,
letting him approach Alanna and Coram. For a
while he said nothing, only stared.

Finally he nodded. "I am Halef Seif, headman
of the Bloody Hawk tribe, of the people called the
Bazhir," he said formally. "Those who are dead were
trespassers on our sands, riding without leave. You
also come here unbidden. Why should we not serve
you as we did these others, Woman Who Rides Like
a Man?"

Alanna rubbed her head tiredly. She felt too
tired and dazed for the dance of manners that
passed for conversation among the Bazhir. Dealing
with these desert warriors was bound to be
tricky; luckily she had learned their ways from an
expert.

Faithful climbed onto her shoulder, setting up a
murmur among the watching tribesmen. Alanna
glared up at the cat, knowing he knew he was
making the Bazhir nervous. *They don't see black
cats with purple eyes often,* she thought. "You're getting too big to sit up there," she whispered to her
pet.

Never mind that, Faithful told her. His meowing had always made as much sense to Alanna as human speech. *Talk to them now.*

Suddenly she felt more confident and alert. "I hope you will deal with us fairly, Halef Seif of the Bloody Hawk," she replied. "We took nothing. We harmed nothing, my friend and I. We are simply riding south. Would you harm a warrior of the King?"

Her gamble failed as Halef Seif shrugged. "We know no king."

Alanna could hear Coram shifting nervously in his saddle. It might have been easier to deal with men who acknowledged King Roald of Tortall. Renegades would not take kindly to the presence of Roald's most unusual young knight.

"You know no king, but others of the Bazhir do. If they knew you held a Knight of the Realm and her companion, they might counsel you to take care," Alanna warned.

This produced some amusement among the riders. Only their leader remained grim. "Is your king so weak he uses women for warriors? We cannot think well of such a king. We cannot think well of a woman so immodest that she puts on the clothes of a man and rides with her face bare."

Alanna pointed to the bodies of the hillmen she and Coram had slain. "*They* did not think I was a worthy opponent either. Can you say that my friend and I would be dead at the hillmen's sword if you had not come? They took my sword from me."

She swallowed hard and said recklessly, "What is a sword? I have my axe, and my dagger, and my spear. I have Coram Smythesson to watch my back, as I watch his."

"Big words from a small woman," Halef Seif remarked. There was no way for Alanna to read his expression.

One of the riders, a Bazhir head and shoulders taller than most of his companions, brought his horse forward, peering at Alanna's face intently. Suddenly he nodded with satisfaction. "She is the one!" he exclaimed. "Halef, she is the Burning-Brightly One!"

"Speak on, Gammal," Halef ordered.

The huge warrior was bowing as low to Alanna as his saddle would permit. "Would you remember me?" he asked hopefully. "I was at the smallest west gate in the stone village that northerners call Persopolis. It was six rainy seasons ago. Your master, the Blue-Eyed One, bought my silence with a gold coin."

Remembering, Alanna grinned. "Of course! And you spat on the coin and bit it."

The big man looked at his chief. "She is the one! She came with the Blue-Eyed Prince, the Night One, and they freed us from the Black City!" He made the Sign against Evil close to his chest. "I let them through the gate that morning!"

Halef frowned as he watched Alanna. "Is this so?"

Alanna shrugged. "Prince Jonathan and I went to the Black City, yes," she admitted. "And we fought with the Ysandir—the Nameless Ones," she said hurriedly as the men muttered uneasily. "And we beat them. It wasn't easy."

A skinny man wearing the green robes of a Bazhir shaman, or petty wizard, threw back his hood. His scraggly beard thrust forward on a sallow chin. "She lies!" he cried, putting his horse between Alanna and the tribesmen. "The Burning-Brightly One and the Night One rode into the sky in a chariot of fire when the Nameless Ones perished. This all men know!"

"They rode back to the stone village, on horses," Gammal replied stubbornly. "And the mare ridden by the Burning-Brightly One was even as this one now—the color of sand, with a mane and tail like the clouds."

While the Bazhir argued among themselves, Coram drew near his mistress. "Now what've ye gone an' done?" he asked softly.

"I think it's more a question of what Jon and I did," Alanna whispered back. "I told you about going to the Black City, didn't I? We fought demons there, and Jon found out I was really a girl. It was six years ago."

"If I'd known I'd be ridin' with a legend, I'd've thought twice about comin' along," Coram grumbled.

"Silence!" Halef ordered them all. He looked at

Alanna. "For the moment, let us accept that you are a warrior of the Northern King, Woman Who Rides Like a Man. Your shield is proof of that. As headman of the Bloody Hawk, I invite you to share our fire this night."

Alanna eyed the tall Bazhir, wondering, *Do I have a choice?* Finally she bowed. "We are honored by your invitation. Certainly we could not think of refusing."

Read all of
Tamora Pierce's

Song of the Lioness Quartet

available wherever books are sold...
OR
You can send in this coupon
(with check or money order)
and have the books mailed directly to you!

❏   Alanna: The First Adventure
         (0-679-80114-6) $4.99

❏   In the Hand of the Goddess
         (0-679-80111-1) $4.99

❏   The Woman Who Rides Like a Man
         (0-679-80112-X) $4.99

❏   Lioness Rampant
         (0-679-80113-8) $4.99

Subtotal.....................................$ _____

Shipping and handling............$ ___3.00___

Sales tax (where applicable) ..$ _____

Total amount enclosed...........$ _____

Name   _____

Address_____

City   _____ State _____ Zip _____

Prices and numbers subject to change without notice. Valid in U.S. only.
All orders subject to availability. Please allow 4 to 6 weeks for delivery.

Make your check or money order (no cash or C.O.D.s)
payable to Random House and mail to:
Bullseye Mail Sales, 400 Hahn Road, Westminster, MD 21157.

Need your books even faster? Call toll-free 1-800-793-2665
to order by phone and use your major credit card.
Please mention interest code 049-20 to expedite your order.